The Murders at Hillside

COMPLETE
DETECTIVE
NOVEL
MAGAZINE

JULY

25¢

In Canada 30¢

by
Virginia
Anne
RATH

PARKHURST

The
MURDERS AT HILLSIDE

The Murders
at Hillside

Virginia Rath

COACHWHIP PUBLICATIONS
Greenville, Ohio

The Murders at Hillside, by Virginia Rath
© 2023 Coachwhip Publications edition

First published 1931
Virginia Rath, 1905-1950
CoachwhipBooks.com

ISBN 1-61646-544-1
ISBN-13 978-1-61646-544-5

I

The Dark House

I have always detested the ordinary weekend, where your hosts insist on entertaining you strenuously every waking instant that you are under their roof. So it was a compliment on my part to Ellen King that I always accepted her invitations. You were expected to entertain yourself at Ellen's; she never invited anyone whom she had not known and liked for a long time; she has an excellent cook and the remains of her father's wine cellar, and Ellen herself was well worth talking to. Therefore, when she phoned, one hot day in July, asking me to come out on Friday with Juliet Selby and Douglas Martin, I accepted without hesitation.

I did not get into Doug's car without my customary prayer that the Providence which had watched over me for nearly sixty years would continue to do so during this ride. The car was much too expensive for him, Doug admitted cheerfully, and added that he had contracted for it on the strength of Ellen's giving him all her legal business.

Douglas was doing very well for a young lawyer in a large city, although he might have been doing better if he had not had an independent streak which made him refuse to be a junior partner in somebody's firm instead of going into practice for himself. I turned over to him everything that came my way, having thankfully retired a year ago from a profession I had never liked and in which I had made a very indifferent success.

It was too bad for Doug's main object in life that Juliet had an independent streak herself. According to his own confession, Douglas had asked her to marry him seven times, but in spite of seven rejections he refused to act the rejected suitor and they were the best of companions.

Juliet was working on the *Tribune,* giving advice to the "lovelorn" and reporting weddings, she said. I don't think she cared for the work as much as she tried to make everyone believe, but, having had her ambitions heartily laughed at, she was determined to make a go of them. Ellen, who had been an old friend of Juliet's mother, didn't laugh, but heartily disapproved. She was equally fond of Juliet and Douglas and was not above a mild attempt at matchmaking by inviting them out to Hillside together. However, this time, Douglas said, she wanted to see him on business. By Juliet's little grimace one could see that she thought this a weak excuse on Ellen's part.

"No, it isn't," said Douglas, as if she had spoken. "Ellen said it was quite urgent, though we would try to combine business with pleasure, and she seemed to be a little upset about something. It couldn't be money matters, because her investments are all gilt edged, so we'll hope I imagined it."

"It's quite a party this time—a family party," said Juliet, without much enthusiasm. "Madeline and Walter are there, and Jack Page, and Mark is home, of course. I don't know where she'll put us all."

Madeline was Ellen's niece, Walter her cousin, while Jack Page was conceded to be engaged to Madeline, though without any official announcement of the fact. Mark was Ellen's half-brother, a likable enough young ne'er-do-well, whom of course she had spoiled, as he was twenty years younger than she.

"They're all harmless enough," I said by way of comfort, not knowing that in a little more than twenty-four
hours we would be all looking at one another with the
furtive glances of hidden suspicion.

"Oh, of course," Juliet agreed. "Only I've reported so
much society the last three days that I was counting on a
quiet country week-end. At any rate, I'm glad to escape
from my bedroom. It's papered in green spiders and is not
a cheerful thing at any time and most of all after a hot
day's work."

"My bedroom is not papered in green spiders or spiders
of any kind," said Douglas insinuatingly.

"Doug, are you making me an improper proposal?" said
Juliet reproachfully. Douglas turned red to the roots of his
red hair.

"You know damn well I didn't—"

"I don't know. I'm only a poor little working girl alone
in a wicked city," said Juliet.

"And well able take care of yourself, I'd say," Douglas
returned, refusing to be baited again. "Never mind, Julie,
you shall have your rest. I'll flirt with Madeline and make
Page jealous." I thought Juliet didn't look too well pleased
with this suggestion.

"I don't imagine Madeline will object," she said. The
best of women are a trifle catty, but the remark was true
enough, as Madeline certainly never objects to masculine
admiration. But Juliet made amends at once by saying with
a half sigh.

"She is so darned pretty."

Well, Madeline is a beauty and Juliet is only small and
slender, with a pale
little face, big dark eyes and a cloud of soft dark hair.

"Oh, she's pretty, all right," said Doug with a significant downward glance at Juliet. "But—"

That conjunction restored him to favor again.

It is seventy miles out to Hillside, which meant, the way Doug drives, a little less than an hour and a half. Hillside village consists of one business street and half a dozen blocks of tree-shaded old houses. The King house does not hobnob with the common herd, but stands on a slight hill several miles from the town. It is a very large, old-fashioned house, once adorned by a cupola. Ellen removed that some years ago and turned the carriage house into a garage. The grounds were always beautifully kept and there are many fine old trees about the place.

Douglas let Juliet and myself out at the front door and drove on to the garage to leave the car. We were admitted by Myra, who looks seventy, but must be about Ellen's age—near fifty, as I know that she had been with Ellen since they were both young women.

Myra's greeting was not ceremonious. She said "How d'ye do" in a grudging tone and waved her hand toward the living-room. "Miss Ellen's in there. You can go in."

Yet we were both favorites with Myra, which was well for our comfort, as she had a most disconcerting way of sniffing audibly at guests she disliked when she waited at table.

Ellen was in the pleasant living-room, turned slightly toward the door with the peculiar "listening" look of blind people. Her cane, I remember, was leaning against her chair, though she did not use it a great deal in her own home. I had not seen her for two months. Perhaps it was Doug's previous remark, but I thought that she did look nervous and unwell.

"I was certain it would be you," she said immediately. "I knew Doug's car and Juliet's footsteps—they are so light. How are you, dear! Sit down and there will be something cool to drink in an instant. The others are at the Country Club. They should be back soon."

Myra brought in a tray of frosted glasses which all of us, Doug having come in by then, accepted gratefully. We must have spent half an hour in the ordinary stupid conversation of the just arrived guests with their hostess, during which time I could see by Juliet's quick glances at Ellen that she also felt that something was wrong. We were just starting to our rooms when a car halted outside.

"Mark," said Ellen at once, and Mark, Madeline, Jack Page and Walter King came in, dusty and laughing.

Madeline, I have said, is beautiful—the Spanish type; shining black hair, deep black eyes, olive skin and crimson lips.

"But," said Juliet to me once with a certain satisfaction, "she has to be careful what she eats to keep her figure. But I must say the result is worth it," Juliet added hastily. "She's the kind that men go crazy over."

Jack Page certainly was mad about her and showed it plainly. Page was a nice enough young fellow, rather well off and rather a neutral type. At least, so he seemed to me; the well-dressed, good-looking enough college graduate one can pick out by dozens in the bond and insurance companies.

Perhaps that was by contrast with Walter King—or Doug. Doug is not half so good looking as Page, I suppose, but he is a tall fellow, beautifully built and that shock of dark red hair and his laughing gray eyes make you forget his wide mouth and rather crooked nose—crooked by reason of being twice broken on the football field.

Walter, however, resembled Madeline enough to be really handsome in a dark, Byronic sort of way. I never cared for Walter, who was inclined to take sullen humors when he was not in a mood of reckless gaiety. Neither did I care a great deal for Mark, a rather spindly young fellow about twenty-one, with a weak chin and a nervous manner of jerking his head and hands about.

When the last arrivals had helped themselves to drinks Ellen came out with us into the hall before we started upstairs.

"We are going to be rather crowded," she explained in her gentle voice. "So, I've put you and Douglas together, Gilbert, if you don't mind. The last room on the left, and Mark, dear, you will have to take the little room on the back stairway. It's all ready for you."

Mark muttered something in an ungracious tone about "stuffy little hole," which Ellen ignored.

"Juliet is to have the middle room on the left side. Dinner will be in about half an hour, so you'll have plenty of time."

"Goodness knows, I need to clean up," said Madeline with a glance at her hands and dusty white shoes. "The sun was broiling on the courts. We'll have to go earlier tomorrow and have a game."

This was to Juliet as they went up the stairs together, arm in arm. Women are peculiar.

Nothing had been changed in the original arrangements of the second story of the house except that Ellen had built on the tiny room where Mark was to sleep and a stairway, which connected with the kitchen below. A rather narrow hall ran the length of the house, broken only by the main staircase.

There were three rooms and a bath on each side; on the left Madeline had the front room, Juliet was next and Douglas and I were at the back. Ellen herself occupied the front room on the other side; Walter was opposite Juliet, Jack Page came next and then Mark. There was no connecting door between any of the rooms except those of Ellen and Walter. This was because Walter's room had once been a nursery and a door had been put in so that Ellen's mother could pass in and out more easily.

There were porches all around the house, and this applied to the second story, too. There was a narrow porch running around the three sides upstairs, on to which all the windows opened. A heavy growth of vines and wisteria climbed to the very windows, and there were several old oaks whose branches rubbed against the rails of the balcony. I have told all these rather tiresome details because later they were of some importance.

Douglas and I settled our things and washed up rather silently. I was a little tired and Doug seemed to be thinking deeply. Presently he said:

"I don't want to seem curious, but just what do you know about Ellen King?"

"Well, she is an old friend of mine, and yet I don't know any more than a hundred other people do, I suppose. I never knew her family. When she was a girl she was in the city for a while, and that is where I met her, through my sister. I imagine her father was something of an old-fashioned *pater-familias*. But I never visited here while he was alive. Ellen lost her sight about two years after I first knew her; she was twenty-four or five them. Her stepmother died when Mark was born and her father very soon after. She came back here, and here she has been ever since."

"Not a happy life," said Douglas soberly.

"No, though she has made it seem so, and I should have said that she was a contented woman—even a happy one."

"So should I—up to now," said Doug.

II

A Scream in the Night

Beside our own party there was only one other guest that night: Edward Trent, who lived nearer Hillside proper and was a retired builder and architect. I had often met Trent at Ellen's and liked him. I think that he was perhaps her oldest and best friend; naturally I had always suspected an old romance between them. I was certain that Ellen could have married had she not been conscientious to a fault.

Outwardly we were a gay party. I kept telling myself that I was foolish in feeling that there was an atmosphere of strained nerves or more than that—dangerous passions—below our lively talk and constant laughter. I had nothing very definite to go on, but Walter's glances toward Madeline disturbed me as well as young Page's resentful frown at Walter's almost aggressively familiar manner toward his cousin.

Mark was sulky, too; about his room, I supposed, as I knew him to be sufficiently childish to resent such things. That was all, until just before we rose from the table, when Douglas said, leaning toward Ellen.

"What about that business of yours, Miss King?"

He meant to speak so that only Ellen would hear, but by that uncanny chance that so often occurs everyone had suddenly fallen silent and his question was heard clearly. Ellen turned her head restlessly, as if she were trying to see her guests on either side of her own place. Then she said in a low voice:

"Not tonight; we'll not talk of it now, Douglas. Tomorrow—tomorrow will be plenty of time."

I went on peeling a large plum, and the faces of the others at that table wore the proper look of polite indifference and lack of interest. Yet I felt, without reason, that Ellen's words had somehow stirred the muddy bottom of a pool and sent murky depths to the top.

"Whenever you say—I'm at your service," Douglas agreed instantly and turned the subject hastily to fishing, which he and Trent discussed at some length without help from the rest of the party.

We all seemed to have turned thoughtful—Heaven knows what were those thoughts—until Ellen roused herself with an obvious effort and began to make plans for the next day.

When we left the table the party broke into groups. Walter said, with a glance at Madeline, that one could see the moon from the porch, and they went out together, Madeline with a teasing side glance at Page, who followed them with rather a grim look about his pleasant mouth. Mark muttered something incoherent about being back in a minute and shambled away. The rest of us sat in the living-room with windows open to the night air, until Douglas, having smoked three cigarettes, became restless and coaxed Juliet out for a walk, probably to propose for the eighth time.

After they had reached the door he turned and came back.

"Looks to me like we're in for a good old thunderstorm," he said.

And indeed the air, which had been growing increasingly sultry all evening, now had a sudden feel of rain about it and the wind was rising.

"Clouds are all banked up on the west, but we'll be back before it breaks."

"Storms blow up suddenly here in July," said Ellen. "I must remind Myra to close all the windows. At least a shower will settle the dust."

That was the way in which we talked for the rest of the evening. I would have been bored at the commonplace stupidity of it if I had been able to shake myself free of the feeling of unrest that had captured me. That Trent was disturbed, too, I could see by his stealthy looks toward Ellen.

A dozen times a question and offer of help was on my lips and as many times I checked it. If I had spoken— But Ellen was not the sort to welcome intrusion into her private affairs, and I thought then that if I had one virtue it was that of minding my own business.

Our dull conversation dragged on with frequent allusions to the weather, for the wind was blowing hard now, and there were faint rumblings of thunder away to the west. The air smelled damp and refreshing when I went to close the windows at Ellen's request, and I said that I would take a turn or two around the porch if they'd excuse me.

I thought Trent was glad to see me go; as I walked back and forth I pondered again on that half-guessed romance.

There was no sign of the younger guests. I decided to walk down to the entrance gate and back, hoping that the slight exercise would help me to sleep. The drive was bordered all the way by trees and shrubs, and I walked silently. When I heard the murmur of voices I thought that it must be Douglas and Juliet and I went nearer, meaning to startle them by appearing unexpectedly. I could see two dim silhouettes behind a clump of shrubbery and then I heard their voices, those of Madeline and Jack Page.

"But Walter is my cousin, silly!"

I couldn't hear Page's voice; he spoke much lower, but Madeline's answer was clear:

"Yes, he's only a third cousin, but my feeling for him is the same as if we couldn't marry. Oh, Jack, I know I'm horrid not to be able to resist teasing and making you jealous. I've done that to all men, but you are the only one I really love. I do love you, Jack! Please believe me—I *do!*"

I don't think he answered in words, but I saw the two dark shapes merge into one as I cautiously turned to go, feeling decidedly guilty, for if ever sincerity was in a woman's voice it had been in Madeline's. Half way back the lane I almost bumped into Walter or rather he into me, for he was walking along blindly and he answered my question with "Where am I going? Oh, to the devil, I guess."

"You'd better come in and have a drink," I suggested.

"A drink? All right, but why stop at one? I'm going to have half a dozen," said Walter, shaking off my hand. "Oh, don't mind me. I'm in a devil of a temper tonight. Ellen shouldn't have invited me down here now."

"Anything out of the ordinary?" I said rather unsympathetically.

"I suppose you mean it's not out of the ordinary for me to be out of temper? I guess you're right, but nothing happens to remove the cause, so what can you expect. Money, the root of all evil—when you haven't got it," said Walter with a short laugh. "I could turn burglar without blinking an eye, if I didn't have a hunch that I'd make a poor one."

There was a closer crash of thunder and, the first heavy drops splashed into the dust at our feet. We made the porch before the thunder sounded again and were joined by Juliet and Doug, breathless with their run from the garden. Trent had gone, and while we were smoking goodnight cigarettes, Jack and Madeline came in. Raindrops sparkled in Madeline's loosened hair and her eyes were glowing. I had never seen her look more beautiful and

Page could look at no one else. Mark had not come, but Ellen appeared unworried and told Myra to lock up, as Mark had a key.

I had been glad to see that Ellen had single beds in our room, as I am a restless deeper. There were bed lamps on the tables and I had helped myself to Ellen's books. I felt that I was going to find it impossible to go to sleep soon and, on my asking, Douglas said that the subdued light would not bother him.

"Nothing like that can keep me awake," he said, punching up his pillows and settling himself with his back to me. In a few minutes he was asleep while I looked at him envyingly.

I read on and on, my wakefulness only increasing. Perhaps it was the storm, as I found myself waiting unconsciously for each volley of thunder and dart of lightning while the rain hit against the windows and the wind tossed the trees about.

The storm drowned out the lesser sounds of a house at night, but I thought several times in a brief lull of wind and thunder that I heard steps passing up and down the hall. This I put resolutely down to imagination, and besides, what business would it be of mine if someone chose to go back and forth even at midnight?

It was just one and I was turning a page when I realized that the storm had subsided a good deal and that there was a strange quiet over the house. In it, I was certain this time, that I heard someone outside. Calling myself a curious old fool, I got out of bed and went quietly to the door and opened it. Our room, remember, was at the end of the hall, close to the short stairway leading to the kitchen. The hall was perfectly dark and I could see nothing, but I could hear someone going slowly down those uncarpeted stairs.

I waited, thinking it might be Mark, coming up, but the sounds died away and I went back to my bed while

Doug slept on, undisturbed. If I had followed—well, we might have been spared those days of uncertainty or perhaps I might not have been here to tell this. I know that I read a page or two more and then I must have fallen asleep, for when I awakened the book was still in my hand, the bed lamp still burning and the hands of the clock pointed to twenty minutes after two. Opposite me Douglas was sitting upright, his red hair rumpled, a startled listening look on his face. Then I knew that what had wakened me was the shrill, horrified scream of a woman.

III

Murder

While Douglas and I still stared at each other the scream was repeated, shorter this time and ending with a horrible choking sound. In an instant we were out of bed and into the hall, which was still almost dark, but before we had groped our way for more than two steps the lights flashed on.

It was Walter King who switched them on, I was sure. He was the first one I saw definitely, standing by the light button at the head of the hall. Then I noticed Page at my side as he came from the room opposite us, breathing hard, his ruddy face a sickly color.

"What is it? What has happened? Where are the girls—where is Madeline—"

But Douglas, without waiting for questions, was already down the hall, and I followed him. Juliet was crouched by the door at the end of the hall that led into the porch outside, huddled into a little heap as if in an attempt to stop the hard tremors that shook her from head to foot. Madeline stood upright, half inside the door, but clutching it as if she needed that support to keep from falling. Her face was colorless and it took two attempts before her lips could form the words she was trying to say.

"It's Ellen, in there—through the window—"

Then I saw that a broad streak of light fell on the porch and out into the night through the open front window of Ellen's room.

"She's— She's— I think she is—" said Madeline and almost fell into Jack's arms.

Douglas stooped and picked Juliet up bodily, thrusting open the door of Madeline's room with his foot.

"Bring her in here," he said curtly to Page. "You stay with them while we—see."

It took all my scanty stock of courage to follow Douglas out to the porch, when he had found by a turn of the knob that the bedroom door was locked. Walter came with us silently, and we looked in at the window, which was half open. The bed was on the farther side of the room, and on it we could see a figure face down, the head half hidden beneath a pillow—and that pillow stained red. An overturned chair lay just in front of the window.

I heard Douglas draw a deep breath; an incoherent expression came from Walter on my other side.

"All right, I'll go in," said Doug, raising the window higher.

We watched in silence as he went across the room, and bent over the bed.

A minute more, and he came back, lowered and locked the window, and wrapping a handkerchief from the bureau about the key, unlocked the door.

We joined him in the hall as he locked the door from the outside, wrapped the key more carefully and put it in his pocket.

"Is it—is she—" I began.

"Dead? Yes—shot," said Doug. "King, would you go down and phone the police, or whoever is the proper authority in this town. We'll go in with the rest and wait."

"There's a sheriff and a town constable. I guess they're the ones. Yes, I'll get them," said Walter, starting down the hall.

I caught myself thinking aloud. "He takes it calmly."

"Why not?" said Doug. "So do we all; that doesn't mean we don't care. Only men don't run around with theatrical exclamations when something like this happens."

"No, you're right. And you mean that I'd better not begin to cast suspicion on anyone?"

"Yes, we'll all be in on that soon enough," said Doug.

We found Madeline sitting up, holding tightly to Jack's hand, her dark, dilated eyes fixed on his face. Juliet was still on the bed where Doug had laid her, a tiny, limp figure. I went to her and I patted her shoulder; she clutched at me, her lips shaking pathetically. "Was she—"

"Yes, my dear," I said as gently as possible, and she buried her face on my shoulder, not crying but still shaking uncontrollably.

Douglas had gone out of the room, to return with a silver mounted flask.

"Here," he said, pouring out a little of the clear brown liquid. "You'd better take a swallow of this. Walter is phoning for the officers and you'll need a bracer before then."

"Oh," said Madeline, shivering. "Will they ask us questions? Do we have to—"

"I'm afraid so. You can wait for them if you'd rather, or if you want to tell us now, we'd like to know how you happened to be the ones to find—this."

Madeline shivered again and closed her eyes.

"Don't talk if you don't want to, darling," said Jack, with a censorious glance toward Douglas. "It can wait—"

"No, of course you want to know. You ought to—why perhaps," said Madeline, starting up, "he—the one who did it is still in the house and we ought to look!"

"I don't think there's any danger of that," said Douglas quietly. "If you mean some outsider."

"But who else? Oh, you don't mean—" Before Doug's grave face she shuddered again and put her hands over her eyes. "But—" she sat upright again, "Where is Mark?"

I suppose we had all known vaguely that Mark was missing, but the direct question had sudden terrifying implications. For an instant there was no answer from anyone of us, then I said as lightly as possible:

"He probably is making a night of it. It isn't three o'clock yet."

Walter came in and slumped down in the nearest chair.

"They'll be right over. Have to get the coroner first. I had the devil of a time raising anyone," he said. "How—how did it happen, Madeline? I mean, that you two—"

"I couldn't sleep," said Madeline. "I had a terrible headache, and I thought I would risk waking Juliet to ask for some aspirin. She was awake, too, but she only had one tablet. I took that, and we sat there and talked—I don't know how long—"

"It was at least half an hour," said Juliet. "We were both restless and wakeful. But the one tablet didn't stop Madeline's headache, so I suggested asking Ellen for more. I was sure she would have some and we knew she was awake."

"You knew? Howl said Douglas quickly.

"We had both heard her go downstairs and back, and we could see the light from her window shining on the porch. So we knocked and told her what we wanted, and there wasn't any answer." Juliet's eyes looked larger than ever in her white face, but she went on resolutely. "We knocked again, and spoke a little louder. But Ellen's hearing was always so keen—and all of a sudden I was panic stricken and I ran out on the porch and looked in—"

Walter ended the silence that followed this by the abrupt question: "Where's Mark?" and Douglas answered, much as I had:

"He's evidently not in yet."

"Have you looked in his room?"

"I didn't think of that. We took for granted— But you're right; I'd better go." There was an undercurrent of alarm in Doug's words that unnerved us all still more, but in an instant he returned, with:

"No, he's not there. His bed hasn't been slept in."

"Probably he won't come in till early morning," I said, but no one answered.

We sat on in the glaring light of all the lamps in the room, a disheveled and unconventionally costumed group. The girls wore those filmy negligees that I had supposed reserved mainly for theatrical productions; Page had stopped to put on a dressing gown and the rest of us were on parade in pajamas. This seemed to strike we three simultaneously, and we went back to our bedrooms for bathrobes and slippers. I remember glancing at the clock again; it was ten minutes of three and I compared it with my watch for correctness.

It had been only half an hour since we were roused by Juliet's screams, and more than an hour since I had heard those footsteps down the back stairs. But if the two girls were right, that person had not been the murderer, for Ellen was alive at that time.

We were hardly settled again in our strained and horrified companionship, when a loud knock sounded through the house and Douglas—odd how he had taken command—went down to admit the officers.

I was greatly relieved by their appearance. I suppose I was unconsciously expecting the overbearing, bumptious type of local officer so much exploited in fiction. I had once met the sheriff, White, before he took office, and he and his wife had known Ellen. He was a tall, rangy man of about fifty, with bright blue eyes and a rather ragged mustache. He owned a good deal of land outside the village, I remembered.

The constable, Jackson, was shorter and stouter, with a pleasant, cleanshaven face that was not lacking in strength and shrewdness. With them was the coroner, Doctor

Grimley. Although I knew him to be an excellent physician, I thought him well named, he seemed so unmoved by the business that he had to do—the only one of the trio who seemed unaffected by this summons.

"You know some of these people, I suppose?" said Douglas, still taking the lead, as no one seemed inclined to speak. Perhaps we all felt, as I did, the inadequacy of words, but the conventions must be practiced even in the face of violent death. "This is Miss Selby, and Mr. Haynes and Mr. Page. I am Douglas Martin—we are all guests here."

White acknowledged the introductions with a hurried nod. "I can't believe it—what King told me over the phone. You say you found Miss King in her room—murdered?"

"Yes, that is true. I locked the door—" Douglas took the key, still wrapped in the handkerchief, from his pajama pocket and handed it to White. "I touched nothing, only made sure that she was—not alive."

"You are sure, then?"

"There isn't the slightest doubt. She had been shot, and I was quite certain."

"Better let me start work then," said Grimley briskly, with a glance at his watch.

White looked at him with a faint tinge of distaste. "All right, in just an instant." He looked at the key. "Good work, that," he commended. "You thought of fingerprints?"

"I'm a lawyer," said Douglas. "Don't suppose there's any point being so careful with the key, but I thought I'd better not slip up on it."

"Good idea not to. We'll get an expert in from the city tomorrow," said Jackson. "Well, chief—"

White started back from an unpleasant reverie, his kindly face lined with responsibility.

"You understand we're not professional detectives, but we'll have to do our best, and I'll have to ask you all to stay in the house until I give you leave to go. We'll go in

the—the room, and look things over. In the meantime, I
think you'd better all go back to your rooms and try to
get some rest until morning. There are a lot of things I'll
want to ask then, and some that I must ask now. First of
all, who discovered this?"

I thought Madeline would collapse at last; she kept
catching her breath in dry little sobs in spite of Jack's
murmured encouragement. But Juliet told the story again,
briefly and without breaking down.

"You knew she was awake! How?" said White, as Douglas had done.

"We heard her go by; at least, I did, and Madeline
spoke of it, too. You see, sometimes Ellen used a cane to
guide her, and she would tap it against the wall to show
her where she would turn to go down stairs. The storm had
gone down, it was very quiet and I heard this tapping and
knew it must be Ellen."

"You heard it too, Miss West?"

"Yes, I—I heard it. I thought it was strange at that time
of night—"

"You looked at the clock?" Jackson interrupted.

"Yes, because I thought it must be late, and it was about
one thirty."

"You didn't go out?" said White.

"Oh no. Ellen—my aunt—wouldn't have liked to know
she had waked us up. And more than that, she wouldn't
have liked me to seem curious."

"But I did go out," said Juliet quietly. "I thought perhaps she wanted something that I could get more easily than she could. I went as far as the staircase and I
could just dimly see her going through the hall, and then I
thought, as Madeline did, that she wouldn't like my seem-
ing curious. Besides, she always liked to do things for herself. So I went back and in a very few minutes I heard her
come back to her room and the door close."

"And that was what time?"

"I honestly can't, say exactly, but I'm sure that Madeline was right and it was around half past one. It couldn't have been more than ten minutes before I heard the door close."

"And then Miss West came over to your room?"

Madeline answered for herself. "Yes, I waited until I was sure I could go without disturbing anyone."

"But you decided after all to ask her for some headache tablets?"

"No," said Juliet quickly. "Madeline didn't want to do that, but I insisted, her headache was so bad. And it wasn't just that—I think I wanted to see if Ellen was all right. I—I was worried. I don't know why—"

"Well, if we take for granted that that was Miss King, the time is fixed between one thirty-five and two ten," said Jackson. "Yet, all of you say that you heard no sounds that might have been shots?"

"We were all asleep except the two girls, I suppose," said Douglas. "Juliet's room is quite a distance from Miss King's, and a silencer makes only a slight muffled 'pop'."

"Yes, it must have been a silencer. What about the boy—Mark?" said White suddenly. "Isn't he staying here now?"

"He went out immediately after dinner and hadn't come back when we retired. We took it that his party was an all-night one."

"Such things have happened," said White noncommittally. "Jackson, you'd better see if you can locate him at any of the clubs or dance halls. Now, I think I'll let you go to your rooms, as I said. Are you young ladies afraid to stay alone?"

Juliet shook her head with a ghost of a smile, but seeing the terror in Madeline's eyes I suggested: "Suppose one of you stretch out on the couch and the other on the bed, and I'll sit here in the easy chair—if that is all right with you, sheriff?"

"Quite all right," said White. Grimley murmured something about "old enough to be safe" and I disliked him intensely.

IV

The Will

All of the first discoveries and proceedings in the room that had been Ellen's for forty years, I learned from Douglas. When the other men had gone into the hall, Doug asked if he could go with the officials, and after a quick, measuring glance at him, White consented.

It was simple enough to tell what had happened and the reconstruction chilled me with horror. I can see how many murders come to be; I can imagine the desire to kill that seizes a man under certain circumstances—but to creep stealthily on that blind woman who must have listened, heard, but could not see her danger, to shoot, and then as she ran blindly toward the bed, to shoot again—no, all imagination fails me there.

I have already spoken of the overturned chair that I noticed in my glance through the window. Under that they discovered her gold knobbed cane and the crochet that Ellen had done so beautifully. She must have been sitting there, quite close to the window, her fingers working in the defiance of sight that had always fascinated me, and thinking. If we could have known what it was that kept her from sleep that night, it might all have ended there, but we have had no way of knowing.

According to Grimley's examination, the shots might easily have been fired by someone who leaned through the open window; the first one a very close shot; the second, when she had risen, overturning the chair, from a longer distance.

"She was sitting quite close to the window," White said, raising the chair and restoring it as nearly as he could judge to its former position. "Odd—on a night like last night was."

"I don't know," Douglas objected. "I have noticed that Miss King was fonder of fresh air than most people. Besides, the storm had died down by then and it was warmer again."

"I suppose so. It must have been from the window, anyway, unless someone raised it, and that isn't likely, as it probably would have frightened her and made her give some alarm, and evidently she didn't."

"The door was locked on the inside, you said? Not that it would prove anything," said Jackson. "It would have been a simple matter to come through the window and lock that door afterward. Are you through, Grimley?"

"All I can do here." Grimley arranged a sheet over the bed—that ghastly gesture of finality. "I'll go down and phone the undertaker to come up with the hearse."

"You can't fix the time of death exactly?"

"Good Lord—no," said Grimley, with some asperity. "Within an hour or two. Between one thirty-five and two ten according to the young ladies. It might have been earlier so far as my testimony is concerned. The first shot went wide, into her armpit. Whoever did it must have been a bad marksman or badly rattled to miss at that close range. I imagine it would have killed her anyway unless she had immediate expert aid. The second shot was through the back, as she turned toward the bed. The impetus of her movement carried her on to the bed, but she must have died almost immediately after she fell. Well, I'll go phone Tom."

Left to themselves, the three men went on with their inspection of the room, taking the utmost care to disturb no article or surface which might hold fingerprints. It was ordinarily a very pleasant, orderly room—the orderliness still remained except for the upset, chair. On a table near the bed was a pitcher of water, glasses and three or four heavy Braille books in a precise stack. Another lay near the edge of the table, *David Copperfield*.

White picked this up, looked at the title and put it down again.

"Might be what she went downstairs for," he suggested. "We've no proof that it was, of course, but the way it is lying here— She must have gone for something."

"I'm pretty sure Myra can tell us if this book was here when she left Miss King," said Douglas. "Perhaps not, but she is pretty observant."

"We'll have her up presently." White frowned. "Funny, none of the servants seem to have been roused by the little girl's screaming."

"Myra and Annie are the only servants, you know, and they sleep in rooms built off the kitchen, and both are rather hard of hearing."

"Yes, it's a long way down to those rooms," Jackson agreed. "A good many closed doors between the back of the house and the front up here, though I would have supposed the screams would have roused them. Well, we'd better go on, I guess this should be opened."

He indicated Ellen's beautiful old mahogany secretary; and lowered the lid carefully, but only ordered pigeon-holes of letters, papers and bills rewarded them.

"Someone will have to take charge of this," said White. "Who is her lawyer?"

"I am," said Doug. "That's why I am here. Wait a minute—" He lifted a large blotter. "The impressions on this are pretty plain—"

"Yes, we'd better keep it," said White, taking it from him.

"But did she write? Jackson objected. "Being blind, I mean."

"Oh, yes, she wrote, all right," said White. "I know that of my own knowledge. I guess she practiced at it a good deal, and she probably took a long time over it, but you couldn't tell the difference from anyone else's writing. My wife had a note from her once about some church affair."

"She used a ruler as a guide; and you can do anything with practice and patience," Doug contributed. "I'll look through all this later. I suppose there is no hurry since it doesn't seem to have been disturbed."

White was closing the lid when Jackson, this time, said:

"Wait a minute. There's something—"

He began to work at the desk lid, opening and closing it, and finally taking out a knife for help, dug out a narrow scrap of paper, which had wedged between the joining of the lid to the rest of the desk.

"This was closed on an edge of paper and it tore off when the desk was opened and closed again. Let's see—"

There were only a few words and parts of the top letters were cut off, but it was easy enough to guess at them.

I, Ellen King, being of sound mind, do this
tenth day—

"A will!" said White.

"Evidently. I'm not surprised," said Douglas. "She didn't tell me what was the business she wanted me for, but I thought that it might be to change her will. She had me bring a number of papers, and her old will was among them."

Jackson put one stubby finger on a word of the writing.

"'Tenth,' you notice? She wrote it last night."

"Yes—" White picked up a hand mirror with a slight show of excitement, and held it close to the blotter. "Let's see what we get here."

The blotting was so crisscrossed in places that it yielded them nothing, but toward the edges they deciphered four significant phrases.

> Fifty thousand dollars—Madeline West, I bequeath—to my cousin, Walter—

And last, diagonally across a corner of the blotter:

> only on condition that—

White drew a deep breath when they had made this out. "Well, it doesn't tell us what the will was, but there's no doubt that she was writing one. I'll keep this as Exhibit A."

"You should have a weapon for Exhibit A," said Jackson. "Let's see, if I wanted to get rid of a gun, what would I be likely to do? Either toss it on the floor and leave it there, or else," he looked toward the porch, "throw it over the railing. I think I'll look around the house when it gets a little lighter."

"Good idea, but supposing your fingerprints were on the gun? said White. "What then?"

"*My* fingerprints wouldn't be on the gun," said Jackson, with an approach to a smile. "They seldom are. If they don't wear gloves they at least wipe off any prints there are. However, we may have to look a long way for the weapon. What's this door?"

I suppose it was because the connecting door between Ellen's room and Walter's was behind a pier cabinet containing old china and bronzes that they had not noticed it at once. However, the cabinet was not against the wall and Jackson was able to examine the door without moving anything.

"Whose room does this connect with? Walter King's? No key on this side of the door—just an old-fashioned hook latch. And," he added slowly, "it's not fastened. The door is locked from the other side."

"The cabinet has stood against the door," White pointed out. "You can see the dents that the legs made in the carpet. It hasn't been moved out long."

"Um," said Jackson. "I wonder—I'm not jumping at conclusions, mind, but it would have been possible for someone to enter this room, and come around to a position near the window. The open window might be a blind, or an accident."

"She would have heard anyone coming in this way much more quickly," said Doug. "Unless—"

"Yes, unless the person spoke, and she knew him—or her," said Jackson bluntly: "Well, let it go, now. Is there anything else to be found here?"

"I don't believe so," said White. "We'll look over things again. It's after four and Mark King isn't in yet. I think we'd better try to get in touch with some of his friends."

"And break the news to the servants."

"Yes. I hate to do that, Jackson. I've been told that Myra has been with Miss King ever since they were girls. Well—" He sighed. "I'd better have a look around this porch. If it was an outsider, he *might* have left some traces."

"Do you think anyone could climb up here by way of these vines?" said Doug, following him.

"I don't know. It's possible, but what do you think?"

"I could do it," said Doug, looking down at the heavy growth of creeper. "But I'd be apt to make some noise and there would be bound to be broken twigs and leaves. I don't see anything of that kind up here."

"No." White sighed again. "And the house was locked. I've tried to think different, Martin; I want to, but it all comes back to the same thing—someone here in the house."

V

Hidden Hates

It was only seven o'clock when we gathered around the breakfast table, most of us desiring nothing but coffee, which was just as well, for Myra and Annie had been told what had happened, and it was an indifferent meal. I may have dozed a little in my chair, but no more than that, and although Juliet and Madeline had been quiet I doubted if they had slept. Walter's eyes were bloodshot; I thought he had already had several drinks. Of Mark there was not even word. White had procured a list of his friends from Walter and called several clubs and roadhouses, but he had not been seen at these.

Jackson joined us at breakfast with the consciously modest look of a man whose reasoning has been justified. Later we learned that he had found the gun with the clumsy looking silencer device still attached, just at the foot of the vines and was reasonably certain that it had been wiped clean of fingerprints. An examination of the grounds had shown no footprints, though the earth was still damp from the rain, nor did the vines show any sign of disturbance.

We all heard the black car draw up, the heavy tread of men bearing an inanimate burden, and the sound of the car driven away again. I suppose we were all relieved, such is the unreasoning fear that so many of us have for the poor clay that is left. In the meantime we were all nerving ourselves for the questioning to come. Myra waited on us, and I did not enjoy the swift vindictiveness of the glances she cast at three of our cheerless party. Once when the door swung open we heard the fat cook's noisy sobbing, but I do not think that Myra had shed a tear.

When breakfast—if it could be so called—was over, White asked us gravely to all step into the living room, the tearful Annie included. We had hardly arranged ourselves in a stiff and formal semicircle when Edward Trent arrived. I thought he looked old and shaken; he had always been one of these dapper appearing, perennially middle-aged men.

"When I learned that Mr. Trent was here last night I thought it was just as well to include him in this inquiry," White explained, sorting some papers. "I suppose you understand that there must be a coroner's inquest Monday, and you will all have to attend. However, we are inclined to make this inquest just a necessary formality—if possible. I think you will all find it pleasanter to answer my questions here, instead of being grilled before an audience. Therefore, if you will cooperate with us now, I hope that the inquest will not be an ordeal for you."

I felt sorry for White, who plainly did not enjoy his official duties, yet found it impossible to shirk them. I had no fear of his questions, but for the others— Well, I suppose that I wanted to know the truth; I would have declared that I did, and at the same time I shrank from what it would be. And yet, looking around in the warm morning sunshine, it seemed impossible to cast aside the idea of some midnight thief; absurd to say that here, somewhere within ten feet of me, sat a murderer. The idea that some of the others might be including me in that category struck me only as mildly humorous.

It appeared difficult for White to begin. I had time for all these reflections before he cleared his throat as a preliminary to speech. "I won't ask you to tell your story of the finding of the body again, Miss Selby, but just a few questions on other matters. Were you related to Miss King?"

"No, not in any way. She knew my mother and always had kept in touch with me."

"Did you think that she seemed in any way worried or apprehensive last night?"

"Yes, I did. Not apprehensive for herself, but a little worried. She was always very cheerful and serene, you know," said Juliet. "And she tried to appear the same as ever, but I'm sure we all felt that something was troubling her. But," forestalling the question, "I haven't the slightest idea what it was."

"Did you see Miss King again after you had all retired?"

"No, I didn't. We said good night at the door of my room. That is, I didn't see her to speak to: I've told you of seeing her go through the hall."

"Could you swear that that figure was Miss King?"

"No, I couldn't," said Juliet, frowning. "It was almost dark, you know. A very dim light burns at the hall door, but she was at the door into the living room by the time I saw her, and her back was toward me. The figure—I can hardly call it more—was Ellen's general height and build and wore a dark kimono and I have the impression that there was some sort of bandeau over her head—"

White looked at Jackson and nodded. It was in such a wrapper that they had found Ellen; the band of dark silk also corresponded.

"You were awake when you heard the sound of her cane?" said Jackson.

"I can't tell if the sound wakened me or if I was already awake, but I think it was the latter, as I had been waking every half hour or so."

"Unless there is something else that you want to tell me, I think that is all," said White. His eyes were on his notes, and he did not see Juliet hesitate before she replied:

"No, I can't think of anything more."

"All right. Now, Mr. Haynes—you were an old friend of Miss King's, I know, and should be able to judge any change in her ordinary spirits. Did you think her worried?"

"Decidedly so," I said promptly. "I was on the point of asking her several times what was wrong, but decided to mind my own business. Old friend as I was, I could think of nothing in the ordinary course of events which should have been troubling her."

"I shall have to ask for an account of the night you spent—" White's tone was almost apologetic.

I smiled to reassure him and told him briefly; that I had read through the storm while Douglas slept, rising at one o'clock to listen to quiet footsteps down the back stairs.

"I thought of following, but decided not to, and went back to bed and to sleep almost at once," I concluded. "Until we were roused a little after two."

White and Jackson were both plainly interested in this.

"You are certain that there was someone?" Jackson insisted. I was a little nettled.

"My room is at the end of the hall, those stairs are uncarpeted, and my hearing is reasonably good," I retorted. "However, do not ask me to deduce whether it was a man or woman or the appearance of the person from the sound of the steps. I don't know."

Jackson smiled politely, unabashed.

"Did any of you have occasion to go downstairs last night for any reason?" There was no answer from anyone, and they passed on to Douglas.

"I am going to ask you to tell me just what you saw when you came into the hall. If anyone thinks him wrong," said White, "he may say so."

"I came out before Mr. Haynes," said Doug. "There was no light except the gleam from the porch, till we had taken a few steps; then it was flashed on by Walter King, whom I saw at the light switch at the head of the hall. I think that Page joined us about then, but I ran forward at once, and saw Juliet—Miss Selby—crouched by the hall door and Miss West standing in the doorway."

"Then Walter King was the first to reach the hall?"

"I believe so. But his room was nearer to the porch than ours," Doug pointed out.

"No one was dressed?" said Jackson.

"We wore night clothes," said Doug dryly. Jackson flushed a little.

"I mean—"

"The two girls, of course, had on what-you-call-'ems—negligées, and Page, who was the last one out, had stopped to put on his bathrobe. Otherwise," said Doug, still dryly, "there was no evidence that any of us had been anywhere but in bed."

He knew, as we all did, that what Jackson wanted to know was whether Walter had been fully dressed.

White resumed the questioning.

"You said that you came down here on business, which you imagined would be the making of a new will. You have no proof of that, however?"

"Not the slightest, yet I am almost certain it was so from vague remarks of Miss King's—and equally uncertain what changes were to be made."

"Can you tell us the provisions of the will?"

"As they were pretty generally known, and the will will be read in a day or so, I might as well," said Doug. "Miss

King was worth about a quarter of a million, all told." I gasped at that, as I should have estimated Ellen's fortune at less than half that sum. "Speaking in general terms, about one-third goes to each her half-brother Mark and Miss West; about half the remainder to Walter, and there is a comfortable sum to Myra and legacies of five thousand to Miss Selby and myself. Mark's inheritance," he added, "was protected."

"Protected? In what way?"

"So he couldn't spend anything but his income," said Douglas bluntly. Otherwise the bequests had no conditions attached." He was thinking of the words on a strip of blotting paper, I suppose, and wondering.

"You think that it was because of the proposed change of will that Miss King

was worried?" Jackson put in quickly.

"What I *think* wouldn't hold in a court of law," Doug said with a slight smile. "But yes, I do. Her finances were in perfect shape; it couldn't have been that."

Jack Page's story took little time. He had, according to himself, gone to sleep at once and slept until awakened by Juliet's scream. He had, as a result, heard no noises in Mark's room next to him, or anywhere else. He supposed Mark had been on a party that had proved too much for him, he volunteered. Asked if he thought Ellen seemed dispirited, he said vaguely that he, didn't know, he hadn't noticed, and didn't know her well enough to judge, anyway.

"Hadn't you been here before?" said the persistent Jackson.

"No, this was the first time. I met Madeline in the city, and we—well—" Jack looked at Madeline half defiantly, half pleadingly, "We became engaged," he finished. "So of course I wanted to come down and meet her aunt."

Madeline smiled, but the look she sent at Walter seemed to me half frightened. If she expected any demonstration from him, she was relieved, for he only smiled in his turn—a queer smile, but so often Walter's expressions had a saturnine quality.

"Miss King approved of the engagement?"

But White cut the constable short.

"I'm afraid that has nothing to do with this business." He turned to Madeline. "Now, Miss West—I believe that Miss King was your aunt?"

"Yes, my mother's sister. My mother died when I was only two years old. We were in Arizona for her health and my father became interested in some mining projects in Mexico and sent me back to Aunt Ellen. He died in Mexico when I was five, so Aunt Ellen brought me up."

"Then perhaps you can tell us more of your aunt's private affairs than the others? I mean, any cause for her death that might occur to you."

"I'm afraid I can't. I can't imagine who—" Madeline's lips quivered, but she pulled herself together with an effort. "It is true that a number of us stood to gain by her death," she said frankly. "But that doesn't seem to me motive enough, because she gave us everything we wanted, you see—she was always so generous. I haven't been here steadily all summer, but when I came three weeks ago, I did think something was worrying her, but I thought it was just an old worry, nothing new."

"And that was?"

Madeline hesitated, then: "I suppose if I don't say this, someone else will. She worried a good deal about Mark. He has always been—well, irresponsible, and apt to be sullen if he didn't have his own way. And lately, as anyone will tell you, he has been running with a very fast crowd, drinking and gambling. Another reason I thought she was

worrying unusually about Mark was because last night she
spoke of sending him away."

"Then you saw her after you had all gone to your
rooms?"

"Yes, I went over to ask her if she had any plans for—
for this afternoon, or if we should just go out to the country club for golf or tennis."

"Was she reading?" said Jackson.

"Reading? Why, no," said Madeline, plainly puzzled at
the question.

"Were there any books there, in her bedroom?"

"There was the usual pile on her table, I am sure. Naturally, I didn't notice particularly."

"None lying open or on the table's edge?"

Madeline frowned. "I'm pretty sure there wasn't. Aunt
Ellen was queer that way; she always put a book back in its
place when she wasn't actually reading it."

I nodded assent to that; it was an oddity which Ellen
and I had in common.

"You were awake when you heard the sound of tapping
which you thought was your aunt's cane?" said White.

"Oh, yes, I had been awake some time, with a bad headache, as Juliet told you. I have heard Aunt Ellen go downstairs before, using her cane to guide her and the noise was
so like that that I didn't think of its being anything else."

"Naturally not," said White. "I think we may take
for granted from your testimony and Miss Selby's that
it was Miss King. Now, as to Mark King—have you any
idea—"

"Oh, I wish I had! I'm sure he—he wouldn't do anything like that, even if he has disappeared.

"Has he ever been missing before?"

"No, the most he has ever done is to come home as late
as six o'clock in the morning, but never so late as this."

White looked at his notes thoughtfully, and Jackson immediately put in: "Had Miss King and her brother quarreled lately?"

Again the question was distressing to Madeline.

"I wouldn't call it really quarreling," she said hesitatingly. "Mark was rather trying, you see, and he was apt to be childish about small matters, but Aunt Ellen always ignored his ill humors, so they didn't actually quarrel."

"But wasn't it rather odd for him to leave after dinner, with guests in the house?"

"It was odd, or impolite, I suppose, but not unusual for Mark to do such a thing."

Jackson persisted.

"But was it not probably because of some disagreement that he left?"

"Oh, I don't know," Madeline seemed on the verge of tears, and Walter interrupted.

"If you want the truth, Mark wanted more money than his sister would give him. He had run up some debts and was being pressed for payment. As to his being angry with her last night, he was sore because she had put him in the little bedroom at the end of the hall when the others came. It was like him to keep harping on that and feeling abused about it, but it seems to me pretty thin as a motive for murder."

"Undoubtedly," said Jackson politely. Whatever his next question would have been, it was interrupted by the sound of the doorbell and he went to answer it, and came back with the fingerprint expert, Mr. Gray.

VI

Questions—And Some Answers

Gray was a dried up, musty little man who looked for all the world as if he might have come from a reference shelf of erudite tomes and be charged out to the borrower with five cents fine for every day overdue. But he proceeded to take our fingerprints with neatness and dispatch and an utter disregard for any wounded sensibilities which this criminal process might engender.

Then Jackson took him upstairs, and until he returned White talked gardening to Juliet and Madeline, and the rest of us appeared to listen with flattering interest, except for Myra, who continued to sit like a brooding figure of vengeance, without raising her eyes from the hard, brown hands folded in her lap.

When he came back, Jackson brought a bulky object wrapped in a towel, which he put on a table and disclosed as a gun.

"Suppose you look at this," he invited, as if it had been possible for us to look anywhere else. Madeline half rose, went white and sat down again. "Have any of you ever seen this gun before?"

The rest of us were spared the necessity of answering by Walter's immediate and careless reply:

"It looks very much like a gun I had when I came here."

"Can you identify it positively?" said White.

48   *Virginia Rath*

Walter gave another glance at the gun.

"Not positively," he said. "It's the same make and model, but that's not absolutely conclusive, and there were no identifying marks on it, as I've not used it a great deal. However, I am reasonably sure that it is mine."

"I suppose you signed for it, and we can trace it by number?"

"Sorry to disappoint you, sheriff," said Walter, almost mockingly. "I bought it from Bill Marx, and he is down in South America. Of course, if you want to locate him, I suppose you can, but it would save you trouble to take for granted that it's mine."

"Very well, and the silencer?" This was from Jackson.

"No, I have never had any occasion for a silencer for what shooting I have done."

"You are not particularly interested in hunting?" said White politely.

"No, though I suppose my friends would tell you that I am an excellent shot," said Walter coolly. "I would not have missed the first time."

If Walter thought that this speech showed a consciousness of innocence I am afraid that by two of his hearers it was put down to utter callousness. There was no difficulty in reading Jackson's expression, and even White looked at him a little sternly.

"When did you last have this gun?" said Jackson.

"The first day we were here we were out in the car and I took it along to shoot at a few rabbits. We came in late and decided not to keep Ellen waiting, so didn't go upstairs, and I tossed the gun in the table drawer here and forgot about it until now."

"Who knew where the gun was?" said White.

"Everyone was present when I put it there, including Mr. Trent who was here to dinner that night. And probably Myra saw it when she did the work."

"Did you?" said Jackson, turning to Myra.

"I saw it early the next morning, but never after that, which means that it wasn't there, or I would have seen it."

"You didn't see it anywhere else in the house?"

"No, I didn't," said Myra briefly.

"In that case," said Jackson, "someone took the gun or it was misplaced three days before the murder?"

"Nearly three, probably," said Walter.

Jackson permitted himself a slight tinge of sarcasm in his next question.

"Were you one of these strangely wakeful people, Mr. King?" Juliet flushed indignantly, and I was not too pleased myself.

"I was not," said Walter promptly. "I went to sleep almost at once and slept until we were all awakened."

I thought he was lying; so, I believe, did Jackson, his next question came so promptly.

"Did you see Miss King after you had gone to your bedroom?"

"I'm not in the habit of visiting even elderly cousins in their bedrooms after ten o'clock. No, I did not."

"You did not open the door between your room and Miss King's and go in to talk to her?" Jackson persisted.

"The connecting door? I did not, and if I had wanted to, it would have been impossible because that door was locked."

"The latch on Miss King's side of the door was not fastened this morning," said Jackson, without emphasis. "Was the door locked in your room?"

"Certainly, and there was no key in the lock." I thought Walter was feeling his way warily, now. "I noticed that, and tried the door, yesterday."

"And removed the key?"

"Removed the key? No, why should I? The key was not in the door when I moved into the room—as I believe I have told you already."

"You noticed that? Why?"

"I don't know. Why does anyone notice one thing and not another?" Walter said impatiently. "What are you driving at?"

"Merely the fact that this key—" Jackson showed it; "was not in the lock at six o'clock this morning, but concealed under the carpet. It was purely by accident that my foot hit against it and I found it."

"About as much accident as when a bloodhound noses something out," said Walter. "Well, I suppose you want to know if I put it there? I didn't—the key was not in the lock at any time since I came."

I thought Jackson would follow this up, but he asked, instead:

"You did not see the gun again, after leaving it here?"

"I did not," said Walter. "But let's say that it was my gun. Also, I had access to Ellen's room, and didn't know it, and I benefit by her will. Am I under arrest?"

"You are not, but I warn you that your manner of talking is not very much in your favor," said White gravely. "We are simply trying to establish and clear up some points. Now, Mr. Trent. Of course you were only a dinner guest here, but I want you to tell me if you know anything which will help us."

"I'm afraid I don't," said Trent slowly. "I left here about nine-thirty—"

"Was everyone in the house then?"

"What? Oh, no. Ellen—Miss King—and I had been alone for about fifteen minutes. Mark was away, and the young people, were strolling about the house and finally Mr. Haynes deserted us to get a breath of fresh air. I left before he returned."

"Did you meet anyone as you went?"

"Yes, I met and said good-night to Miss Selby and Mr. Martin. I went through the garden, as my shortest way home is a path that strikes from there, over the hill."

"I don't like to pry into any personal affairs, Mr. Trent, but you have known Miss King longer than anyone here, except Miss Bell. Do *you* know of anything—"

"I do not know of anything—such as you mean. We talked of the merest commonplaces all evening, as Mr. Haynes can tell you."

"That is true—while I was here," I said cautiously.

"But you were alone for fifteen minutes, Mr. Trent— and old friends—" Trent merely closed his lips in a straight line, unresponsive to White's suggestion. White frowned and went on:

"Mr. Trent, you are an architect, I believe! Do you know anything of the structure of this house?"

"Something, yes," said Trent, surprised. "It was built over fifty years ago, however."

"So I understand. I hope you won't think I have been reading too many detective stories, but do you know of any way to gain secret entrance to this house?"

"I must say such an idea had never occurred to me." Trent's answer was rather amused. "Within my knowledge no such entrance, or any secret room, exists."

"You met no stranger, or anyone else, on your way home?"

"After I left the garden I met no one during my walk home."

"Did you think Miss King worried about her brother?" said Jackson.

"Yes, I—the fact is, I knew that she was," said Trent, "as Miss West says, she was thinking of sending him away from companions who were doing him a great deal of harm."

Annie, the cook, would have been glad to talk more than she was required to, but she had nothing of value to tell and White soon cut her short. She had been with Ellen for four years; she slept in one of the two rooms built off the kitchen, always slept "like the dead" and had done so last night.

Yes, she was a little hard of hearing; so was Myra, and if they were asleep, even the sound of a scream from upstairs wouldn't be apt to wake them.

Yes, she and Myra did all the work—this rather resentfully—though when there was this much company they usually got Nelly Boggs to help out in the daytime. And who there was would want to kill a lovely lady like Miss King, she didn't know, but— As I said, White cut her off, pleasantly enough, and turned to Myra.

"New, Miss Bell—" I confess it was the first time I had thought of Myra's having a surname, or known what it was. "You have worked—lived here, how long?"

"I have been Miss Ellen's maid for over twenty years." Anything more unlike the usual conception of a lady's maid than the gaunt, wrinkled Myra can hardly be imagined. "I am Mrs. Bell, not Miss," she added indifferently, "I came here when my husband died."

"You knew all the family, then?"

"Yes, such as was living here."

"I see. Then perhaps you may be able to tell us more than anyone else here has—of any possible reasons for Miss King's death?"

"I don't see no *reasons*," said Myra harshly. "She was a saint on earth—helping and looking after all of them around her like she did, and none of them were grateful for it, but wanted more all the time."

"If you have anything definite in mind—"

"I have plenty that's definite," said Myra, with a glint in her deep eyes. "I mean her closest relatives; the ones she brought up and paid their way. There isn't one of 'em that's not glad she's dead and they've got her money—"

"Myra!" This was Madeline; Walter only smiled.

"Yes, I mean you, Miss Madeline, and Walter over there. She treated you like her own children and you went sullen if she didn't hand out money like a mint, or crossed you in anything."

Madeline shrank before the woman's look as if it were a physical blow.

"Miss Bell, I can't let you speak this way, unless you know of something that actually happened," White broke in. "You have no right—"

"I've got the right of one who loved her," said Myra. "As to anything happening—all they've said about Mark pestering her for money and even threatening her if he didn't get it—"

"Threatening her? In what way?"

"With killing himself. But he wouldn't do that—Mark ain't got the nerve to kill himself, let alone her. But there was others. Mr. Walter King," Myra's formality was contemptuous, "Mr. Walter King was anxious to tell you about Mark wanting money, but he didn't say he wanted it twice as bad himself, and come down here just to get it. They talked about it, too, several times, and she finally told him he had no right to ask money from her, that way, and she'd cut him off altogether if he didn't stop and settle down—and let Mark alone."

"You mean Mr. King influenced Mark King?" said Jackson quickly.

"I guess you'd call it that—drinking and card playing."

Walter, who had been unmoved through all this, in contrast to Madeline's indignation, threw one leg over the other and said negligently:

"After all, Mark was of age. If not with me, he'll be with someone else less scrupulous. As to my wanting money, I always want money, and I was willing to take what Ellen would give me now and forfeit any future claims I

might have. Also, I'm interested to know this old busy-
body's authority for the conversations she says took place
between Ellen and me."

For an instant I thought Myra would rise and strike
him, but she answered sullenly to White's question:

"I couldn't help hearing a few things when people talk
at the top of their voices in the middle of the day when
there's work to be done."

"No doubt you could be trusted to do all your work
near the keyhole," Walter drawled.

"I guess anyone here knows I don't snoop—no more
than I stopped going about the house the usual way unless
I was ordered not to. As to Miss Madeline, here, she was
forever bickering with Miss Ellen about one thing and
another—"

"I don't have to answer such insinuations," said Madeline, with flashing eyes. "But I'm going to— Naturally
my aunt and I disagreed on some subjects; I'm young and
she was nearly fifty, so how could we think alike about
everything? She didn't like some things I did, just as she
disapproved of what she called 'the younger generation'
and sometimes we disagreed about those things. And Myra
thinks like Aunt Ellen did, of course, and thought I should
always do exactly as she wished. That's so, Myra, isn't it?
Isn't it?"

"I suppose it is," said Myra reluctantly. "But it didn't
make Miss Ellen any too happy."

White diverted the channel of the conversation hastily. "Were you with Miss King last night—I mean, do you
usually help her get ready for bed?"

"Always, and last night was the same as ever. I guess I
was with her about twenty minutes, and then I went down
to bed myself."

"Did you meet anyone on the way?"

"No one."

"You went straight to bed?"

"After I'd seen that all the doors and windows were closed, and locked. I always look after the locking up."

"You are sure they were locked?" said Jackson. "The doors, of course, but what about the windows? Didn't you leave them open in the summer?"

"Not downstairs. There's been a little stealing now and then around here, and last night it was raining, so I was carefuller than usual to see that the windows were locked."

"We'll look them over when we have time," White said, in an aside to Jackson. "See how good the locks are. Now, Miss Bell, you have heard all that was said about the connecting door between Miss King's and Walter King's rooms. Was that always locked?"

"I never knew it any different," said Myra, "And that tall cabinet always set up against the door in Miss Ellen's room, and it was in place when I left her last night."

"You're sure of that?"

"Of course I'm sure. Miss Ellen was particular about things being in their place, so I'd have noticed anything being out and put it back again."

"Did you look after all the bedrooms?"

"Yes, that was my work. The key on the other side of the door was in Mr. Walter King's door yesterday morning."

"But he says it wasn't."

"Maybe he didn't look very careful or forgot," said Myra maliciously. "The key was there, where it's always been."

White put his next question hastily, before Jackson could speak. "You said Miss King was particular about the arrangement of articles. Do you know if she had the book *David Copperfield* with her when you left her last night?"

"Not that one. She had a stack of four books on a table, but *David Copperfield* she was reading downstairs in the afternoon. It was on the table when I went through the

sitting room last night, because it was open and I closed
it. I thought it was funny she hadn't put it up like she
always did, but I didn't put it away because I thought maybe she wanted it again."

White nodded. "Did Miss King always use a cane to
guide her?"

"Not very much—hardly any. She got around wonderful. But she used it on the stairs sometimes being as she
stumbled once going down there."

"Did she often wander around the house at night?"

"I don't know what you call wandering," said Myra
curtly. "If she wanted something in her own house, she
went and got it. She hadn't been sleeping well lately—
though she was never very good at sleeping. Only it was
more so last week."

"You slept all through the night?"

"I was tired from the extra work," said Myra, as if
excuses were necessary. "I guess I wasn't awake once."

"Er—did Miss King confide in you—or do you know of
any happenings in her past life—"

"Miss Ellen wasn't one to tell things to a servant and
there wasn't anything in her life for her to be afraid of
people knowing," said Myra tonelessly. She was looking
at her hands again and did not raise her eyes at White's
"Thank you."

VII

A Door Slams

We were all exhausted by this time; mentally more than physically. "I feel squeezed as dry as a sponge," said Juliet with a rueful smile. White and Jackson had gone about their investigations of the house, Trent had declined to stay for the luncheon Myra and Annie were preparing, and the others had left Juliet, Douglas and myself to go out on the screened section of the side porch where it was cooler.

"What next?" I said, as Juliet curled up wearily on a couch and Doug sat down beside her.

"The inquest Monday, if nothing happens before then." Douglas was so preoccupied as to be quite unlike his usual companionable self; his lawyer's mind already sifting and turning over evidence.

"Do you think they can hold Walter—or will?" I ventured.

"I don't know. Oh, they can hold him, all right, but I think White sees it wouldn't be wise—yet."

"He wanted money pretty badly. We had a conversation to that effect, but I didn't bother repeating it."

"Good for you," said Doug. "As to money, don't we all benefit from Ellen's death, except you, Trent and the cook? Even Page, indirectly, if he marries Madeline. He's well off, of course. As to me, five thousand dollars means a lot,

besides what I'll get for settling the estate, and that will
be a large sum."

"I can give you an alibi," I said, half seriously. "You
slept like the dead."

"You can't alibi me between one ten and two ten," said
Douglas. "No, the fact is that any of us had opportunity,
except Juliet and Madeline, and suppose that it was someone else that Juliet saw—"

"But I'm sure—" Juliet began.

"So am I." Douglas smiled at her. "I was merely point-
ing out improbabilities. Except for you two, any of us
could have done it, and if the shot was fired from the
porch, what would be easier than stepping from a bedroom
window and going around that way, instead of risking being seen from the hall?"

"Have White and Jackson thought of that?"

"I don't know, sir. I suppose so, but they've a lot to
think of at once. All they kept back from us that I know of
was the evidence of a new will. He told us of that."

"But she wasn't cutting Walter out, according to that,"
said Juliet.

"No, but that phrase 'on condition that' interests me,"
said Douglas. "Of course, that may have been attached to
anyone's bequest, we don't know whose. But I would like
to—also what our precious fingerprint expert is discovering."

"Do you believe in fingerprints?" said Juliet a little
scornfully.

"Well, I believe black is black and white is white," said
Douglas. "And I've seen a number of men hanged by fingerprints, so I don't care much about having mine found
in incriminating places like the handle of a gun."

White came to the door just then with a friendly nod
for all of us. "The fingerprint man is through upstairs,
Martin, so any time you want to look through those papers
you're free to go in."

Douglas sighed and got up. "I suppose I'd better go at them right away, though I won't have much time before lunch. I'll make a starter, though."

He was gone, Juliet looking after him. "I could do worse than marry Doug, couldn't I, Uncle Gilbert?" she said unexpectedly.

"You certainly could. I don't see how you could do better," I said. "And it would be very easy for you, now."

"Oh, don't!" said Juliet. "I know, and it's so horrible to think that because Ellen is dead things are easier for us. Yet I can't be sorry about the money just by itself—"

"She wouldn't want you to, and she always hoped you and Doug would marry, so if it comes about through her—"

"I know. And Doug is nice. He's almost as nice as you, Uncle Gilbert."

This was rank flattery, and I said so.

"No, I mean it," Juliet insisted. "I can't help comparing you two with the others. Even Jack Page, who is nice enough in his way, seems sort of soft beside Doug. But I think Madeline really loves him."

"I'm sure of that. Even born coquettes fall in love once in a lifetime," I said sententiously.

"Only she's led Walter too far," Juliet went on, as if thinking aloud. "And he's desperately in love with her. It almost makes me afraid—"

"Afraid of what, child? After all, what can he do? If a girl flirts with a man a little too much and then refuses to marry him, what is there to do but smile and take it?"

"Depending on the man, there's several things he might do," said Juliet. "And Jack is beginning to resent Walter's attitude; he smiles about their engagement as if it was a joke. We're in enough trouble without all this. Uncle Gilbert—"

"Yes, my dear?"

"I wish we knew more about Ellen's life."

"But, as Trent and Myra said, it was utterly blameless, and uneventful so far as I know."

"I can't help it, call it feminine foolishness if you want. I prefer to call it womanly intuition," said Juliet with something approaching her usual smile. "But I do feel that the key to this thing lies farther back than we think. And Myra might know, or poor Mr. Trent, but if they do they wouldn't talk on the rack if they thought what they had to tell discredited Ellen in any way."

"It was fortunate that White refused to let Myra go on as she started," I said. "As it was, her accusations were sufficiently widespread. I expected her to turn on me any moment with a scathing denunciation because I was so fond of old Mr. King's port." Juliet rewarded this very mild joke with a smile, as White came to the door again.

"I just had to see a reporter from town, and I gave him as little information as I decently could. I suppose there will be a flock of them soon, but I'm asking everyone not to talk."

"Reporter? Oh—heavenly days!" said Juliet. "I'd forgotten—"

"Forgotten what?"

"That I'm a reporter myself, Mr. White. But I never report anything but weddings, and I'm on a vacation, so you needn't worry about me."

"You're different from most of them, then," said White, with the conviction born of experience. "Usually they don't know what the word vacation means. But a little publicity may help us to find Mark King."

"Look here," I said. "Do you think he—"

"I don't know," said White wearily. "By all the rules I suppose we ought to consider his disappearance at such a time very suspicious. But from all they tell me of him, he might just have gone off in a fit of childish sulkiness. We have no proof that he ever entered the house after he left

it. Of course, he had access to that gun, but so did everyone else, and from what I've seen of Mark King I can't
imagine him capable of such a murder. However, on the
face of it, it doesn't look any too good."

Luncheon was announced, and we went in. Someone
had invited Gray to stay and he did, tucking away an
amount of food that I marveled at. Evidently he was hun-
gry from his work upstairs, but he contributed nothing
to the talk unless his manner of masticating lamb chops
could be called conversational.

Jackson's chief contribution to the aforesaid table talk
was that the windows in the front rooms showed no signs
of having been tampered with. He made this statement
without comment, but we all understood its implications.
It was after that that Walter broke the surly silence he had
maintained since coming in.

"Do we have to stick around the house all afternoon?"

"If any of you want to go down to the village and will
tell us, it is all right," said White gravely. "I hardly thought
any of you would."

"Don't worry, I'm not going down to talk to any of the
town busybodies," said Walter rudely. "I wanted to take a
walk. If you've anyone you'd like to send along with me, I
haven't any objections, but I'd prefer having him with me
to behind me."

White let that pass, though Jackson's square jaw set a
trifle. "There is nothing more we need you for, until this
evening. Perhaps when Mr. Gray has finished his work we
will have more questions to ask." It was almost a threat, in
the politest kind of way.

"I'm going to go on with those papers," said Douglas.
"You'll find me in the den—I believe Mr. Gray is going to
use the library?"

Gray signified with a grunt that he was, and returned
to his consumption of charlotte russe. I think he must

have had several large cavities in his teeth which created
a suction when he ate soft desserts. We left him and the
two officers still drinking coffee, though it was fairly hot
now. I went into the library for books, intending to catch
up on sleep if possible, but fortifying myself against wakefulness. Madeline went upstairs, Page sprawled out on a
couch and seemed to go to sleep instantly, while Walter
lounged away out the front door.

Coming from the library with my books, I met Juliet
just turning from the telephone in the hall. Her eyes were
snapping.

"Uncle Gilbert, did I say this morning that I was a reporter?"

"I believe you did," I said, somewhat mystified.

"Well, 'was' is correct tense. I was a reporter, I'm not
any more." Juliet looked vindictively at the wholly innocent appearing telephone. "Do you know what that was?
The sacred *Tribune,* wanting a story! They were pleased because I happened to be here and behind the scenes. Oh—I
could have slapped the fat, vulgar thing!"

"What did you tell him?" I asked somewhat unnecessarily.

"I told him to go to hell!" said Juliet and marched upstairs.

In my own room I took off my shoes and coat and
stretched out on the bed, closing my eyes resolutely. But
my brain seemed determined to work whether I wanted it
to or not. Ellen—old friends—how few of them were left.
And she was the last one who remembered the girl whom I
once hoped to marry. Was Juliet right and there had been
hidden secrets in that outwardly calm life? What had been
in that will she had drafted last night? Walter—Mark—
Trent—they all swam together about me in a wheeling ka-
leidoscope and I finally slept.

When I wakened, it seemed the most natural thing to have started up, listening—as if all my awakenings were to be with the sudden start of fright. It was after six; I must have slept all afternoon, and the shadows were lengthening. For an instant I thought my first impression of being roused by words and voices was a mistaken one; then I heard a woman's hysterical voice in the front hall and reached hurriedly for my shoes.

Juliet joined me as I reached the staircase, her white dress evidently just flung on hastily, and Madeline, following her, had not stopped to change her loose robe.

"I don't know," Juliet said, in answer to my question. "I was so tired that I was still sound asleep. I think it's Annie—"

It was Annie, weeping noisily now and trying to talk through a constant succession of hiccoughing sobs. White stood over her awkwardly, venturing now and then to pat her shoulder, while Douglas and Jack Page stood by in mingled amusement and curiosity and Myra in open scorn.

"Something scared her," White explained. "We were all sitting around and everything was quiet when she burst in here with a yell, and I haven't been able to get a straight word of what it was out of her."

"I'm telling you straight enough, if you'll listen," said Annie wiping away her tears with her checked gingham apron, her double chins quivering. "The door just started to open slow and easy like an' when I give a yell it closed to again with a slam—an' my heart ain't strong an' I can't stand much more of this place!"

"What door?" said White patiently.

"The door into the furnace room, down in the cellar." Annie was growing more coherent in her anxiety to prove that she had heard something. "I come into the kitchen to start dinner an' I thought first off I heard steps movin' around somewheres, but being nervous I told myself I was imagining things. Then I thought I'd open some cherries, but there wasn't any upstairs, so I started to go down cellar for them, an' it was then that the door started to open like I said—slow and easy. I just give a yell, and then it closed with a little bang and I come a-running in here."

"It may have been the wind," White began. "Do you think—"

"I think we'd better look without any more waste of time," said Doug. "If there was someone there he's had about ten minutes to get away. Page, you'd better stay with the girls."

VIII

Mark's Return

The kitchen was a huge, old-fashioned one with what seemed to me a bewildering number of doors. Two, close together, led into the hall and onto a back porch, another into a pantry, still another to the two rooms built off a tiny passageway for the servants, while one was the entrance to the back stairway. I tried to draw the plan of the room, but as I am no architect I found that none of my stairways looked as if it was going anywhere.

A short flight of very steep steps, sunk in the floor, led down to the cellar—the old-fashioned way of building. A dropped pan and dish towel were mute evidence of Annie's sudden flight, but otherwise everything was spotlessly ordered.

White tried the door tentatively, but it opened easily under his grasp. The cellar, dark and large as the kitchen, with the odor of stored vegetables and fruit hanging over it, was almost uncannily quiet.

"There must be a light button somewhere," said Douglas, coming after White.

He fumbled about the walls while I stayed at the head of the steps, waiting. Suddenly he froze into attention, hand still outstretched.

"Listen—what's that?"

The light was dim, but we could see the great cold bulk of the furnace, the rows of bottles and canned fruit and the vegetable bins. In the corner next the furnace were seven or eight large boxes, and a pile of old sacks, which stirred strangely.

We listened for an instant and thought we heard nothing but the sound of our own breathing—but there were only three of us, and there was a fourth drawing moaning breath in that cellar. Doug renewed his search for the lights desperately, but it was I who saw the button in the kitchen and pressed it.

Douglas was over to the furnace before either of us, and throwing aside the sacks, disclosed the body and bloody head of Mark King. I found myself staring from that to a red-encrusted hatchet and back again in horrible fascination.

"He's not dead, but he's damn near it. We've got to get a doctor here in a hurry. I'll go after one myself if you can't get him on the phone at once. Hold that door open, please."

Douglas was lifting Mark gently and quite easily. I pulled out my handkerchief and spread it over his face.

"No use frightening the girls," I explained. "It looks rather—terrible." It was a poor excuse for my own shaken nerves, but Doug accepted it

"We'll have to take him to Miss King's room. There's no other ready and it's the best one, He may have to be moved later, anyway," said White. "I'll phone Grimley, and get the women out of the hall."

I don't know how he broke it to them. I heard Madeline's sharp cry as I followed Douglas upstairs and helped him lay Mark on the bed. It had been freshly made, but in an instant the pillow was stained red—again. I stood there thinking of Ellen's head against that same pillow, and praying that I was not going to forfeit Doug's good opinion by acting like a hysterical woman. Busy settling Mark's thin body and loosening his clothing, he did not notice me, and I had time to take a grip on myself.

"That's all I dare do," he said, straightening. "I'm afraid to move him around. Did you get the doctor?"

"He's coming as fast as he can get here," said White, standing in the doorway. "You're a good man to have around, Martin. I stopped to lock that door; key was on the other side. I want to go back down there as soon as Grimley comes. See here, where's King—the other one?"

"I don't know," said Douglas with a little tightening of his lips. "I haven't seen him around there all afternoon. He went out for a walk, you know."

"I know he said he was going walking. When that woman screamed, I was standing at the front door for an instant. Jackson had just left with Gray, to take him to the station. You came down out of that room they call the den, and Page from downstairs and Myra—where was she?"

"In the garden picking flowers. All present and accounted for. Then the three who had been sleeping upstairs joined us. I take it that you had been asleep, sir."

"Yes, all three of us. We didn't wake up until she got in here and began to carry on. Page was just coming downstairs?"

"So he said. It would have been very easy for whoever was in the cellar to come out and go upstairs by the back way," White pointed out. "But we have no reason to suspect any of you who were there. Even Page, whose appearance was certainly somewhat—er—"

"Timely?" Douglas suggested.

"Yes." Mark stirred and moaned. "And," White ended, "it would be even easier to go away by the back door and not come into the house at all until later."

There was the sound of a hastily driven car stopping before the house. White went to the window and looked down. "Yes, it's Grimley now, and he has a nurse with him. We might as well go down; there's nothing we can do here." Douglas and I went into the living room while White took the doctor upstairs. It was almost a replica of another scene. Jack sitting by Madeline with a protective hand over hers; Juliet by herself on the big Chesterfield. Douglas went over and sat beside her. "All right now?"

"Oh, yes," said Juliet steadily. "Was he—"

"He is still breathing, but that's about all."

"But what—what happened?" said Madeline, her voice shaking. "Mr. White only said that Mark was hurt."

"Someone tried to cut his head in with a hatchet," said Douglas. I thought he was brutal purposely, and Page turned a sickly white. "We don't know why—yet."

"And we don't know why Ellen was killed." Madeline began to whimper a little. "I'm afraid—perhaps someone is trying to kill us all—"

I heard Jack murmur something about "protecting" her, and to save my soul could not keep from smiling. Page was a nice young chap, but somehow I could not see him in the role of stalwart protector.

At this moment Myra thrust her head in at the doorway.

"That worthless Annie is having hysterics in her room, and wants the doctor when he isn't busy. I wouldn't bother him, myself. I'm getting something to eat, and you'd better get dressed to be ready to eat it," she said, addressing herself to me, but with an unfavorable glance at Madeline's negligee.

But Myra's meal was a little delayed, after all, for White came in, and seeing that the others had gone upstairs, asked Douglas and me to go down to the cellar with him. I would rather not, but Doug assented willingly, adding with a quizzical smile:

"Don't you know your professional dignity demands secrecy?"

"I'm not worrying about my dignity and I'll take all the help I can get," said White. "You've some brains, and being a lawyer— By the way, did you find anything important in those papers?"

Doug shook his head. "Not a thing. They were all old business documents; nothing of a personal nature among them. You know, I can't help wondering—"

"What?" We were going down the cellar steps again how, with Myra watching us sourly. White unlocked the door and we stepped in. "What?" he repeated.

"If she had some other place for her private papers— personal ones. Of course, she may not have kept letters. Being blind, she must have had someone read them to her—By Jove!" said Douglas, stopping in the middle of the stone floor. "I never thought of that."

"You mean, someone must have read all her letters for the last twenty-five years?" I ventured.

"Exactly. I wonder who it was."

"Myra?" I said.

"Perhaps, some of them. Or Trent."

"Probably," White agreed. "But both of them are tight mouthed propositions, and you can't dig information out of people with general questions. Those are the only kind that we can ask, because we haven't the slightest clue to what they might know. Well, here we are."

White bent over and studied the floor around the furnace intently before he straightened up, with:

"Nothing here. Stone floor and no dust. I'd say, though, that he must have been standing near the furnace when he was struck, because if he'd been dragged or carried any distance there would be blood. He could have fallen right beside these sacks—" White was lifting them from where they had been scattered as he spoke.

"Yes, there's a large stain," said Douglas. "When he fell there was nothing to do but shove him over a little more and throw the sacks over him."

"Must have thought he was done for, or they got excited or frightened by something and didn't dare to stay to be sure."

"Well, if Annie hadn't decided on cherries for dinner this might have been successful," said Doug.

"It may very well be yet. Grimley isn't too hopeful. But if he can talk, our problem is solved—unless," said White, "he was hit from behind."

"He was—once. That may not have been the first blow."

"But what," I said impatiently, "was he doing down here at all?"

"It must have been last night," said White, not answering my question directly. "Those weren't fresh wounds. Mr. Haynes, I'd like to know myself what anyone was doing in this place in the middle of the night."

"This furnace door isn't quite shut," said Douglas absently. Then: "Wait a minute, White. If you wanted to burn some papers without risking someone's seeing you, or having detectives discover the ashes—"

"By jiminy, you're right! Miss King's draft of her will— huh? But if young King was burning that, who tried to kill him?"

"What makes you think *he* was burning the papers?" said Doug.

"You mean he caught someone else at it, and they tried to avoid discovery that way. Yes, that's maybe more reasonable," White said. "Though—there's that woman Myra. I've just been thinking that I didn't *see* her in the garden a while back. If she found him here and knew— But it's pretty fantastic. Only, what was young King doing here at all during the night?"

"Oh, I think that's easy enough," said Doug. "He had a key to the front door that Ellen gave him, and a key to the back door that he got for himself. His regular room was a back one, and it was sometimes more convenient for him to go up that back stairway. Say that he came in this way last night, heard a sound in the cellar and came down."

"All right," White conceded. "And those two maids slept through it? Still, I suppose if this door was closed—it's pretty heavy, and the door into their quarters, it's reasonable enough. But I'm going to try how far a dull thud and reasonably low voices carry out of here, when Myra's not in the way. Now suppose we look around here a bit."

It was Doug's younger and sharper eyes that made the only discovery; two torn bits of paper which had drifted across the floor and half under a box.

From their shape they were evidently parts of a paper which had been torn diagonally several times, and it was impossible to make out more than a few words in places. Luck was with us in one way, however, for almost at once Doug fitted the two pieces together. As to any sense that the thing made, it was quite hopeless, but we puzzled over it nevertheless.

"That isn't Miss King's writing?"

"No, I never saw it before—have you?"

"Never," I said. "I wonder why it should have been burned?"

"It might have been an accident," Doug offered.

"It looks as if those personal papers I wondered about must be accounted for, now. Probably everything of that kind was taken."

"It sounds like an ordinary letter telling about some friend's health, or approaching death," White mused, studying the scraps. "'She'—that must be she, though part of the capital is missing. 'She is worse—quite hopeless.'

she is worse,
it is quite hopeless
uickly or longer
 it is impossible
t home or around
 appreciate all
tainly it was
 t and had we
 o   hasty you would
ne to warn us.
I do not care; but
            we

I'm inclined to think that you're right, Martin, and it was simply included with the will by accident. Still—"

"Yes, that's it. I'd keep it."

"Don't worry," said White. "I'm keeping it, and anything else that comes my way."

When we came into the kitchen we found Myra waiting. "Your food's ruined, while you've been doing your detecting," she informed us scornfully. "Are you ready now?"

"All ready, and I'm sorry we kept you waiting," said White pacifically. "By the way, Myra—do you dust all the rooms?"

"Every morning—dust and rub down the furniture."

"Then you did that in Miss King's room yesterday?"

"Certainly I did."

"A good job?"

"I always did a good job in Miss King's room particularly," said Myra, assembling food and dishes. "I dusted everything in that room. 'Scuse me; I want to get things on the table. The others is waiting."

IX

A Letter from Ellen

We invited White to come upstairs with us and wash up—Jackson, he said, had gone home to dinner.

"Lucky my wife is away just now," he said, reaching blindly for a towel at the old-fashioned washstand in our room.

He was one of these men who always cover themselves largely with lather when washing and then dance about with soap in their eyes, groping for an elusive towel. Doug thrust one into his hand; he freed himself of soap and went on:

"I think I'll stay here tonight. I'll sleep on the Chesterfield downstairs. If young King comes back, all right, but if he doesn't, I've got to find him. I should never have let him go, but I didn't have much to hold him on—then."

I wanted to ask the natural question but I was spared the necessity, for as Douglas took his turn at the washstand, he handed me a letter, with:

"Know that writing?"

"Certainly; it's Ellen's," I said instantly.

"Go ahead—read it. It's an interesting little document."

I read in that precise writing of Ellen's which was so remarkable considering her disability:

My dear Walter,

I have listened to your last letter and do not care to answer you fully, now. You have no right, I remind you, to expect more than I care to give you. I might also recall to your mind that I have been very generous, again without having to, and my generosity seems to have been of little profit to you. Things must go differently with you from now on, if I am to continue to be so.

As to Madeline—I am very sorry you feel as you do about her, and I am perhaps to blame for having allowed you to see so much of each other, but you know quite well that I have never encouraged you to think of each other except as cousins, and indeed had no idea that you did so. Even if I were willing, and there were no other considerations involved, Madeline would not wish to marry you, and if she did I would not give my consent.

I am willing to talk things over with you when you come; in fact, I want to come to a thorough understanding with you. But do not attempt to bully or threaten me, or we will not get far with our discussion. And I will not have my guests annoyed with scenes; we will speak of this privately or not at all, and you must leave it to me to find the time and opportunity for our talk.

Doug had been reading rapidly over my shoulder. "Well," he said, "that isn't so terribly damaging, is it?"

"Son, I've noticed you sticking up for this fellow, without having any particular liking for him," said White. "Is there any special reason for that?"

"No, except that here we are—six of us who know each other fairly well and were guests of Miss King's. Things would be even more difficult if we began hurling haphazard accusations at one another. I'll admit that there are a number of things not in Walter's favor, but I think that if he came to trial a good lawyer would probably get him off."

"Yes, on the evidence you *know,*" said White. "You don't consider that letter important?"

Douglas shrugged his shoulders.

"I suppose it is, more or less," he conceded. "It proves that Walter had been bothering Miss King for money; that she wasn't satisfied with his way of living and that there was to be a showdown during his visit. All of that we know, anyway, if we can accept Myra's testimony. As to his feelings for Madeline, that's fairly obvious to anyone who has eyes."

"Yes, I can see that for myself," said White. "And I agree, with you—this letter established just the things you mentioned. Here's the question—did anyone know what business you came here for?"

"I didn't know for certain, myself," Douglas began.

"But it was mentioned at the dinner table that night and Ellen said that she would wait till morning to talk with Doug," I said. "I thought at the time, though you understand I haven't the slightest proof, that several members of our party understood what she was intending to do, though nothing was said about wills."

"Which ones did you think knew of it?"

"Well—Mark, Walter, possibly Madeline, and Trent," I said reluctantly.

"Exactly. Now, gentlemen, here's the joker. You heard Myra tell me that she dusted and rubbed the furniture every morning, so fingerprints made on its surface would not remain from the day before. Well, Gray naturally found Miss King's prints, also Myra's, about the bureau, table and other articles; Miss West's in one place only, and Walter King's on the desk and table. Gray said that their position indicated he was standing and leaning against them in both cases. But he said he did not see Miss King after all of you went to bed!"

"Perhaps in the daytime—" I began.

"No, because they were gone all day until dinner time, and while Walter King was here Miss King was not in her room. He might have entered it when she was absent, which is not exactly favorable to him, either. I want very badly to see King and ask him a few questions," said White grimly.

"Were there fingerprints on the cabinet before the door?" Douglas asked suddenly.

"Yes. Miss King's—and Walter King's," said White. "Hers seemed to prove that she was the one who moved the cabinet, his seemed as if made accidentally in passing it."

I could see by Doug's expression that he still did not consider the situation hopeless.

"It's a bad business when a suspected man lies and is caught at it," he said. "It shakes everyone's faith in all that he says, even what happens to be true."

"And where," I asked, prompted by a trifle of malice, "did you find Ellen's letter to Walter?"

White looked a little uncomfortable. "That was Jackson's work," he said. "He was combing King's room this afternoon. That's one reason he was willing to let him go. Jackson's a smart man and he does these things better than I do. I believe he'd pick a man's pocket if he thought there was something in it to help him find the truth."

White sighed.

"He's not been here as long as I have, and it doesn't go as much against the grain to ask personal questions and bully all these people, like it does with me. He's had more experience, anyway, used to be with some mounted police force—" He stopped in sudden consternation. "Good gosh! I forgot Myra's dinner. I'll bet she kills us—"

If looks could slay, Myra's, when we entered the dining room, would have done so, for we were delayed still farther by meeting Grimley in the hall.

"Can't tell," he said, in answer to White's question. "He may live, but the chances are that he won't. If he does, it's a hundred to one he'll never be wholly normal or remember what happened. In any case, there's no use you even thinking of trying to talk to him for a long time, and the house has got to be kept quiet. I'm leaving Miss Barnes in charge; she's capable, and she'll call me if she needs me. I can make it in less than ten minutes if it's necessary. If there's nothing more, I'll be getting back."

"The cook has hysterics," I suggested.

"Let her have 'em," said Grimley unfeelingly.

As I said, when we entered the dining room Myra's looks were murderous, but the others did not seem to care. The meal, in spite of having waited so long, was excellent, and to my surprise and with a slight feeling of guilt, I found myself doing full justice to it. We were about halfway through when the door was pushed open and Walter walked in.

I think we did not know whether to be relieved or regretful. After all, it would have been simple had he not come back. And he must have come very near slipping away that afternoon, but his curious streak of recklessness brought him back to his dear cost.

That he had been walking was evident, for his clothes were dusty and he looked hot and tired.

"What's up?" he asked immediately. "I met a starched female in the hall, who told me to be very quiet, and the place smells like a hospital."

"It is a hospital for the time being. Mark King is upstairs with his head nearly smashed in," said White. "In all
probability he won't live."

"Good Lord!" I thought Walter for the first time was
genuinely moved. I think he had a few stirrings of con-
science with regard to Mark. "Was he—where—"

"In the cellar. He would probably have laid there long
enough to die if the cook hadn't heard someone in the cellar and caused us to go down there. While she was having
hysterics in the front hall the—er—intruder got away,"
said White, buttering a biscuit lavishly.

"Oh—I see," said Walter slowly, and with his customary careless insolence. "So I am expected to prove an alibi
for that time, is that it?"

"We'll discuss that—and other things—later," said
White, with a glance at the two girls.

Madeline frankly abandoned her previous pretense of
eating, and I felt my own appetite failing. As earlier in
the day, Juliet, with a violent pretense of nothing wrong,
talked gardening to White. She knew nothing about it,
she said, but had once had to put out the house and garden column for a week, and indignant subscribers were
still writing in to complain of her advice. Walter simply slumped sullenly in his seat and stared moodily at his
plate for the rest of the meal.

I think White must have murmured a suggestion to
Juliet, for presently she excused herself and Madeline went
with her after one frightened glance around at us.

"All right, let's get on with it," said Walter, lighting
a cigarette with unsteady fingers. He had been drinking
too heavily and the results were beginning to be apparent.
"What have I to account for now?"

White tossed the letter down before him.

"Is that yours?"

Walter gave it a careless glance.

"I thought it was, but apparently I am mistaken. It seems to be public property."

White ignored the open sneer. "Did you and Miss King have the interview that she speaks of?"

"According to Myra, we did."

"And the results were?"

"Oh, she refused to shell out any more unless I straightened up and got a job. As to what she writes about Madeline," said Walter more slowly, "that hasn't anything to do with it. Even if she had approved—it was up to Madeline. I didn't know about Page when I wrote to Ellen."

"Did you know Miss King was going to change her will?"

"I didn't think she was, though she spoke of a possibility of making changes later on. But by God!" said Walter, flaring up unexpectedly, "I can't see why I'm to be subjected to this endless questioning. You can stick me in a cell when you want to, but I'm sick of this, and I'm damned if I go on with it!"

"I think you will—here or in court," said White sternly. "This is what I want to make clear to you. You denied having seen Miss King last night, yet your fingerprints were found in that room in three places. How do you account for that?"

Walter did not answer and Douglas leaned across the table toward him.

"Look here, Walter—he's got to ask these questions, and if you answer them here you may not have to answer them somewhere else. Consider I'm your attorney, if you say so, and that I've advised you to answer."

"Oh, all right—I guess it doesn't matter much," Walter muttered. "Yes, I saw Ellen last night. She let me in through the connecting door."

"And you talked about the will?"

"I've said I didn't know about any will," said Walter impatiently. "We talked money, as usual, but we didn't row about it this time. She said she'd give me a pretty fair sum when I'd held a good job for three months, and I could pay up what I owed. That was all—I went back to my own room, heard her drop the latch on the other side and locked the door myself. Next morning, I got to thinking, and so I hid the key the first chance I got. It was a crazy thing to do, but I could see what was coming and I lost my head and acted like a fool."

"And that is your final story of the night?" said White in his most noncommittal manner.

"Well, if I think of any changes, I'll let you know," said Walter with a mirthless smile. Certainly he had a genius for saying the worst possible thing for himself.

"Where were you this afternoon?"

"Walking—and sitting under a tree, thinking. No, I have no witnesses to prove my statement," said Walter. "I went along the brook at the foot of the hill, and I was around Trent's house a good while."

"Trent's? Why?" said White, surprised.

"To see what he was doing. I didn't see him outside the house but once, but that once was interesting. You'd like to know about it yourself."

White would have liked to, but he could see by Walter's smile that he did not intend to tell. "We have no proof how the man—or woman—in the cellar left, or where they went," he began.

"What—no footprints?" said Walter. "Thoughtless. Every criminal should be compelled to leave at least one good set of footprints about the premises. Well, is that all?"

"All—except that I advise you not to leave the house again without permission."

Walter scowled, but he left the room without comment. It was only half past eight, but most of us expressed a desire for bed, and Douglas and I brought down blankets and pillows for White's comfort. Jackson rang up while we were doing this, to say that he had better spend the night in town, and he and White had a long conversation over the phone.

Douglas and I were just going up when we met Miss Barnes in the hall with a pitcher of water.

"He's resting quietly," she told us. "It's too soon to know anything definite, of course."

She was a stalwart woman with a pleasant face and an air of dependability which made me glad to have her in the house.

"Well, look after him carefully. It's mighty important to us," said White. "Good night, everybody."

So our second night at Hillside began.

X

The Locked Doors

I think I have already said somewhere that I always had prided myself on a certain ability to mind my own business. When I record some of my actions during our time at Hillside, I do not feel so inclined to boast. I seem always to have been hearing things not meant for my ears—not only overhearing, but listening shamelessly. Perhaps that was because everyone but Juliet and Douglas considered me quite harmless and rapidly approaching senility.

I was tired enough that night to fall asleep instantly and sleep heavily for several hours. Then I awakened, as was to be expected, intermittent sleep being one of the penalties of approaching old age. I felt quite comfortable and drowsy and Doug's steady breathing was a reassuring sound. I wondered what time it was, but was not sufficiently curious to turn on the light to see, and there was no moon.

After several moments of lying in this pleasantly somnolent state, my attention was caught by the sound of voices. I could not be sure of their location, but my first thought was that Mark was worse and help might be needed. I got out of bed carefully, not to wake Doug, and went out into the hall.

The door of the room where Mark lay was closed and I could see a thin thread of light beneath it. It was from

Jack Page's room opposite ours that the voices came. I hesitated for a moment, then I stealthily stepped nearer and for the first time in my life applied my ear to a keyhole.

Page was talking; I caught the end of a sentence. "—so I've warned you! I've stood it as long as I intend to!"

"Just what have you stood?" Walter's smoothly ironical voice.

"Your behavior toward Madeline! It's insulting to both of us, and cousin or no cousin, I don't intend to have any man looking and acting toward her as you do! Is that clear?"

"Sufficiently. Better let Madeline give her opinion before you go too far, though."

"I am voicing Madeline's opinion, too. She loves me and your conduct is embarrassing to her. She's fond of you and she's afraid that you'll make matters worse if she is rude to you. Well, I'm not afraid to be rude to you, or of your tantrums because you can't have what you want, and I've given you a final warning!"

"End of act two, curtain falls with noble hero defying villain," Walter jeered. "Well, if that's all you've dragged me out of bed to hear, I'm going back—"

I retreated hastily to my own room; then, holding the door open just a crack, heard Walter's door shut softly. Then I looked at the clock for a brief instant by the small light over the desk. It was eleven and I made a mental note of the time, having an uncertain idea that it might be important, before I dropped the old-fashioned bolt on the door, wondering vaguely as I did so at the absence of a key.

Back in bed again, I found thankfully that my brain was literally too tired to think about what I had just heard, and I drifted back to sleep with the hope that there would be no more awakenings. But there seemed no peace in that house on any night, and I found myself starting up as I had once before, listening intently. As before, I became aware that Douglas was sitting up, too. His voice as it came to me, was strained: "Quiet!"

I listened, and heard it—the soft tapping sound of a cane coming nearer and nearer. We were neither of us superstitious men, but in the dead of the black night that muffled tapping was indescribably awful and unexplainable. I was gripped by a cold chill and Doug's nerves were shaken so that it was a full moment before he leaped to the door. The bolt dropped and then he pounded against the wood savagely, and swore.

"Locked! White! White! Damn it all, man—wake up! We're locked in! White!"

As he shouted, the tapping had ceased. There was the sound of a choked, gasping cry, and a thud; then the answering voice of White from below.

"I'm coming—the damned lights are out! What is it? Who called?"

"Here—it's Martin. The door is locked and there's someone outside!"

We heard White running heavily up the stairs, then a sound as if he stumbled, and his voice again: "Someone out here—it's a woman! Where's the key—"

Ignorance of who the woman might be made Douglas quite wild, I think. He drew back and hurled himself at the door. It groaned and cracked under his weight and a panel gave way at a second impact. He found a chair in the dark and finished it with that. I followed him into the hall through the splintered wreck. White was kneeling there trying to strike a match with fumbling fingers. The light flared up briefly and illumined the white face of Madeline West. There was a slight trickle of blood across her cheek, but she stirred as the match I flickered out.

"I don't believe she's hurt, just stunned some—" We could hear Juliet calling to us now; Page was hammering at his door and the steadier tones of Miss Barnes came to us. "There must be a key somewhere," White said desperately. "Here, take some of these matches."

"Sweetheart, are you hurt? Are you all right?" This was Douglas before Juliet's door, and we could hear her faint answer:

"Perfectly safe, Doug. I've closed the windows and locked them."

"Just a minute. We'll find a key." He struck another match and began a frantic search in which White and I aided. We found a key in the lock of Page's door, and as we had supposed, it fitted all the locks. Doug unlocked Madeline's door first, lifted her and carried her in to the bed, while White released the others.

"We've got to get some lights—what l has happened to them anyway—"

"I don't know. They went out about half an hour ago, and I lighted the lamp I had brought up because I knew something like that happened sometimes," said Miss Barnes. "Wait, I'll bring it out."

In the pale yellow circle we all felt more at ease, but every one of us was noticeably shaken. Walter's face was haggard in the dim light and Page had a queer greenish look about the mouth. I suppose the rest of us cut scarcely a better figure.

"There's another patient you'd better look at, in there," said White, nodding toward Madeline's room. "She must have—"

"You mean Madeline—she isn't—she may be dying!"

White, cut Page short. "She's all right, just hit alongside the head," he said, not unkindly, "She may have done that falling. Can you all stay here minute while I get some lights? We've got to have them."

"All right," paid Doug. "We'll stay here, but I'd see if the switch in the basement is all right if I were you. They might have been turned off there."

"I'll do that. If they're not, I'll bring back some lamps or candles."

We all drew closer together as he disappeared down the stairs. It seemed hours, but it was in reality a very short time before the lights flashed on in the room where Mark lay, and we were able to turn them on in the hall and in all the other rooms.

A minute more, and White came back, still carrying the lamp, and followed by Myra in a most respectable gray wrapper.

"She was just getting up—thought she heard something," he explained briefly.

"I thought I'd better bring this lamp back with me. The front door was open and I found this in the hall." "This" was a yard stick tipped with steel ends.

"Front door open?" Douglas repeated. Miss Barnes had left us to go to Madeline, but the rest of us remained in the hall. "Was it locked when we went to bed?"

"I locked it myself," said White. "The key was on the floor."

"And I looked to be sure you'd done it," said Myra, without the remotest idea of being humorous.

"You didn't run into anyone when you started up here?" Doug asked.

White hesitated, "No, I didn't meet anyone, but I had a notion I heard someone close to the house start away. What I don't know, yet, is how the whole thing started."

"Someone went along this hall, tapping against the walls with that," Douglas nodded toward the stick. "I don't know how many heard it, but Mr. Haynes and I did."

"I didn't—it was Martin's yelling that woke me up," said Page. "Then I heard someone fall—" He shuddered, looking towards Madeline's room.

"I was asleep, too," said, Walter shortly. "The shouting woke me, too." I thought I detected the faint odor of whiskey on his breath again.

"I heard the tapping—I was lying awake. It seemed to paralyze me," said Juliet, "I couldn't move or call, or even think what it meant—"

"But what could be the object?" White began.

"Well, you see how it affected all of us," said Doug. "On the face of it the thing seems simply a malicious freak meant to terrorize us, but perhaps there was something more back of it than that."

"Rather a great risk to take—"

"With the lights out and the doors locked," said Juliet, with a tremulous smile. "Whoever it was, got away safely."

"But these doors—haven't they keys on the inside?"

"No, they all have old-fashioned sliding bolts," said Juliet. "Any key will fit all the locks and Ellen said once that bolts were safer. No one ever thought of being locked in from the outside, though I think some of the doors had outside keys."

"Do you know what ones did?" White turned toward Myra.

"The rooms we didn't use so much; the little room where Mr. Mark King was supposed to sleep last night, and if I rec'lect rightly, there was one to Mr. Page's and Mr. Haynes's doors."

"And anyone of them would lock all the doors?"

"Certainly—the locks are all alike."

"And none of you heard the keys turned?"

"I think now that I must have," said Juliet. "Something waked me before the tapping began. It was such a slight noise that I put it down to nerves, but it might have been that."

"And you, Miss Barnes?" said White, as she came out of Madeline's room.

"Well, no, I didn't." She appeared just a trifle embarrassed. "I'm afraid I dozed a little," she admitted. "After the electric lights went off it was hard for me to keep awake. I kept falling asleep and jerking awake again at the least noise. A little sound like that might have had that effect without my knowing what the sound was. Oh yes, I heard the tapping, and I was still trying to decide what it was when it stopped and Mr. Martin began to shout. Miss West is all right now, sir, and she wants to talk to you."

Madeline managed to smile at us, but her lashes drooped wearily and her words were halting.

"I'm all right—yes, Jack, I really am. There's just a little cut on my cheek. I'm thankful it wasn't what it—might have been—" She stopped and drew a deep breath. "I was awake, you see, and I heard this sound. At first I couldn't think what it was, and then I decided it sounded like a key turning in my lock. That seemed foolish to me, but I got up and tried the door—and it was locked."

"I was in an absolute panic. It was awfully foolish, but I felt I had to get out of that room or go mad, and when I couldn't turn on the lights it was worse than ever. Then I thought of the front window onto the porch and I went out that way and around into the hall as quietly as I could. I had just reached that when the tapping began, and I could feel, more than see, someone going slowly down the hall. I—I—"

"Darling, don't talk any more tonight," Jack begged. "You can tell us tomorrow."

"Certainly, Miss West, if it upsets you to talk," said White kindly.

"No, you want to know, of course. It was just remembering—how I felt when I heard that sound. I wanted to scream and I couldn't. Then it came to me that it must be *somebody,* and I was afraid to make a sound. I knew I mustn't let him get away, and I thought if I slipped down the hall to Jack's room and opened the door and called—I didn't know everyone was locked in. I didn't think I made any noise while I was trying the I door, but he must have heard, because before I could utter a sound something struck me—"

"And you didn't get the slightest glimpse of him?"

"No, I couldn't see anything. I think I grabbed at him as I fell, but I'm not even sure of that."

"All right, Miss West. We won't bother you any more tonight. It was mighty plucky of you, at that. I'm going to camp in this hall the rest of the night, so don't worry."

XI

Before the Inquest

It gave us all a feeling of security to know that White was keeping watch in the hall, which would have been sadly shaken had we known that Doug found him placidly asleep when he stole out at six o'clock. He merely grinned to himself, however, and went down to do a little illicit investigation.

One day's heat had already baked the earth again, but Doug, looking for footprints in the best sleuthing tradition and without any expectation of finding any, was rewarded. In two places in the garden where overhanging foliage and recent watering had kept the ground damp, he found a man's tracks leading away from the house. Jackson and White afterward verified this find, and Doug's opinion that this man had been running.

The cellar yielded nothing to any of them except the fact that it was an easy matter to turn off the lights at the switch. Douglas came upstairs then, as silently as he had gone down, and discovered a key lying among the splintered wood from our door, and another key in the door of the little room at the end of the hall. This door, however, he discovered to be unlocked and he stepped into the room. No one had been there since the officials had visited it the day before, and everything seemed in place, except for two things which Doug noted and reported to White.

"The window was up, just a little. I tried it," he added inconsequentially. "And it is apt to stick at that point. And there was a chair standing out of line as if someone had brushed against it in passing and almost knocked it over."

"All of which means—what?" said White.

"Well, we were all rattled last night and didn't have time to think, and that open front door needs to be accounted for, too. The same with those footprints. But on the other hand, the locked doors don't eliminate any of us from the possibility of having staged last night's performance."

"I had got around to thinking about that," White said. "So long as that one room wasn't locked, it would be easy enough to step out on the porch and down to the room and in through that window. And the same thing would work, getting back. Hang the architecture!" he added. "If it wasn't for all these porches we'd be a lot better off."

In return for Doug's relation of this to Juliet and myself after breakfast, I told them of the conversation I had overheard between Jack and Walter.

Douglas chuckled and Juliet said severely:

"Uncle Gilbert, I'm ashamed of you. You couldn't have heard them unless you were very close to the door."

I had tried to evade this point, but I had now to admit rather weakly that I had been quite close.

"But I don't see that it is so important," Juliet went on. "That is, so far as this crime is concerned. We all know that Walter is wild about Madeline and that Jack resents it."

"True," I said. "It simply adds another complication, and it is interesting to know that those two were not asleep all night, as they implied."

"It was twelve-thirty when the disturbance occurred," said Douglas. "Likely they were asleep then."

"Very likely," I agreed, without conviction.

"You don't think so?"

"Well, do you?" I countered. "Or you, Juliet?"

"I think that Madeline has at least an idea who struck her down in the hall," said Juliet slowly. "I don't think she knows, and so long as she's not sure, she isn't going to tell. I think she still has the fear that perhaps the whole family is marked out for extermination."

"The one who staged that performance last night is not necessarily the murderer," said Doug. "But if caught his actions would be hard to account for."

"I can't account for them, anyway," I said. "They don't seem sane."

"No, I don't think they are," said Juliet quietly.

"You mean?" I began.

"Exactly. I think whoever is responsible for this must be a little mad."

The idea was not a comfortable one and I would have preferred to reject it. "Aren't all murderers a little mad?" I suggested.

"Oh, no," said Douglas. "Some of them are simply practical to the highest degree. But still, I have to agree that what happened last night doesn't seem to fit into a sane scheme of things."

"Unless there is treasure buried in the walls and the tapping was to find the hollow spaces," Juliet suggested so gravely that we both made the mistake of accepting her suggestion seriously, until she laughed at us. "You poor dears have been reading too many detective stories," she said.

"Not me," Douglas returned grimly. "This satisfies me very well without adding any fiction. Here we are, three at least reasonably intelligent people, and we're not advancing at all. We're supposedly on the inside, too."

"That's one trouble, we're prejudiced," said Juliet. "If we made up our minds to face whatever we might discover and then went ahead for all we were worth—"

"I'm game if you are," said Doug. "As a matter of fact, I have been going ahead as much as I'm able. What about it, sir?"

"You may wish you hadn't," I said.

"Truth is better than uncertainty," Juliet flashed, and Douglas nodded. I was of the opinion that while uncertainty may be uncomfortable, truth is sometimes crushing, but they were both young enough to prefer to risk the latter and bound up again.

"Go ahead, and count on me for any help I can give, and please consult me before you do anything rash," I said.

They agreed solemnly, and then suffered a rather ludicrous reaction when they were unable immediately to think of any course of action sufficiently heroic to end the uncertainty which they condemned.

"After all," said Juliet, in disgust, "what can we do? We've no right to hold an inquisition on all the people who *might* know something?"

"No, but I would like to have some of them in the witness box with power to handle them without gloves," said Douglas.

"Undoubtedly the rising young attorney would wring the truth from their lips," Juliet mocked. "Well, I'll tell you all something I think, but have no proof of."

"Womanly intuition again," said Doug, repaying her in kind.

"Nothing else but. Anyway, I shall follow this up because I'm the only one who very well can. Myra offered to stay with me last night, though Madeline certainly needed her more than I did—"

"She has always liked you," I said.

"She has nothing against you two, either, which is more than you can say about her and everybody here. But what I started to say was that I got the impression last night and this morning that she wants to tell me something, but is afraid to. I don't mean afraid for herself, but that what she might say wouldn't be to Ellen's or the family's credit."

"Does your intuition extend far enough that you can give us some idea what she *might* reveal?" said Doug.

"Not the slightest, except that I think it is something in Ellen's past life that we don't know. I hate that expression 'past life,'" Juliet broke off to say. "But what else can one use? Another thing, Myra used to think quite well of Mr. Trent, for her, but now I believe she is suspicious even of him. I think that is absurd—" Juliet stopped again and flushed at Doug's reproving headshake. "No, that's the wrong way to go at it, isn't it? Well then, it is rather improbable that he, of all people, would kill Ellen. What do you think, Uncle Gilbert?"

"It certainly seems so. I would have said offhand that Trent was one of these one-woman men."

"She should have married him, if she wanted to," said Juliet. "Her blindness wasn't any reason for not marrying, but she was so dam conscientious."

"I can't see Trent as Ellen's murderer, either," said Douglas. "But I'm not sure that he doesn't belong somewhere. You know, those footprints can't be disputed, and unless we're going to drag in some mysterious outsider, Trent would be my first choice for that intruder. Those prints were in the garden—"

"Near the footpath he would take to go home?"

"That's it, Juliet. If he was the one in the hall," said Doug slowly, "I can think of one explanation, but it is too blamed fantastic."

"Go on; we can stand it," said Juliet.

"All right, suppose he did try that tapping stunt on the theory that the murderer was among us and the sound might break his nerve?"

"I've heard worse," said Juliet. "Rather stagey, but so was the whole episode, though it didn't seem so when it was happening."

"If the one who made the footprints had nothing to do with what happened upstairs, then I'm stumped," said Doug. "He must have been here for some reason, and I have no idea what. But I do think that it is a mistake to ignore Trent, as they have done since yesterday morning."

"Hasn't anyone let him know about Mark?" I said.

"I don't believe so. It's only common politeness, too, so I'll do it, and if I don't get him to come over here, it won't be my fault."

"He must have heard by now," said, Juliet. "News doesn't keep long around here. He should have come."

"It would have been rather late before he could have heard," I suggested. "Give him time. It's not long after breakfast. One thing I would like to know, since we are all airing our pet curiosities. What did Walter see Trent doing yesterday that he thought interesting?"

Doug groaned. "He might have been doing anything from standing on his head to burying a bone."

"And whatever it was, we're not apt to get it from Walter," said Juliet. "Unless it is something that will help to save his skin."

"You think he's going to need something like that?"

"Well, I wouldn't be surprised, Uncle Gilbert. No telling what Jackson has been doing all this time. They'll have the coroner's inquest tomorrow," said Juliet. "Doctor Grimley said he thought it would be best to wait, because they might have to consider two murders instead of one. I think he's a beast."

"That was a crude way to put it, but he was right," said Douglas. "Miss Barnes just told me that although Mark is quiet enough he is in a heavy stupor and may never come out of it."

"I know. I think Madeline and Jack went in. I didn't—I can't help the poor kid any by standing over his bedside, and I'm so tired."

"Swell rest you're getting," said Doug indignantly. "Can't you take a nap now?"

"No, I don't think so. This afternoon, maybe. Never mind," said Juliet, "I shall have a vacation when they let us go, and before I start on another job."

"You're sure you lost your old one?" said Doug eagerly.

"Well, if I haven't I'm the first person who ever told Connolly to go to hell and got away with it. And if he tries again to get me to help out his darn old circulation, he'll get left again, so I think I'd better be thinking about a new position."

"Listen, Juliet—before you do that—"

I got up immediately and discreetly faded from the room, knowing that Doug was probably about to propose for the eighth time. He did not look gloriously uplifted when I next saw him, telephoning to Trent, but neither did he appear at all perturbed, so I supposed that Juliet at least had not been very harsh.

Myra was passing through the hall at this moment with her inevitable dust mop in hand, and I stopped her. "Myra, will you answer a question for me?" I said as ingratiatingly as possible. I have always been a little afraid of Myra.

"Well, you can ask it if you want," she said with only her customary ungraciousness. "I'll answer it if I see fit."

"Did you read Ellen's letters to her, all these years that she's been blind?"

"Some of them I did. She'd ask me what name was on them, or the postmark if there wasn't a name, and if she wanted me to read them, she'd say so. Otherwise she'd keep 'em, and I wouldn't be offended, though she knew I'd never breath a word of what was in any of them to *anyone.*"

"I'm sure you wouldn't," I agreed promptly, and ventured another question. "Do you suppose Mr. Trent read the others to her?"

"He might have. I couldn't say," said Myra impassively. "She didn't get so many, anyway. I got to be about my work."

She stopped to admit Jackson before she went into the living room. He and White talked in the hall for a few minutes, and as they made no pretense of lowering their voices I made none to keep from overhearing.

"Yes, I found out where Mark King was night before last, not that it helps us much now," said Jackson. "One of the waiters remembered him being at the

Country Club with a party. I went around to one of them—young Elwood—and he says Mark left some time around one, but he isn't sure just when. However, that's near enough to be reasonable. Elwood says Mark seemed a little out of sorts at first, but was perfectly cheerful before he left."

"With some of that cheer these youngsters carry in their pocket flasks, I suppose," said White. "Well, poor kid— Did you follow up my other tip?"

"About Trent? Yes, I saw the cook this morning, and she had only one thing to tell me except that Mr. Trent is a 'gr-r-and' man. He burned a large armload of papers yesterday afternoon in the incinerator in the back yard."

"Did you look to see—"

"I did," said Jackson. "But there wasn't even a scrap left, and I'm still smelling of burned garbage. And where does it get us? A man has a right to burn anything he wants in his own yard."

"At least we know what King was talking about," said White. "Now, this front door. I want you to look at it on the outside and tell me what you think. The key was on the floor, as I told you, so it must have been poked out of the lock from the other side, but if I'm not mistaken that would be perfectly possible with a long, pointed instrument like a file."

They withdrew to the porch, leaving me to the morning papers for entertainment, if garbled accounts of the "mysterious tragedy" could be termed entertainment. I was solacing myself with the comic strips when Douglas came in to tell me that Trent would be over soon.

"And I'll swear that he didn't want to come—not that I blame him. But he's too much a gentleman not to," said Doug. "Just the same, I'm going to be impertinent as hell, and ask him two or three things."

"Such as?"

"Wait and see," said Douglas provokingly.

However, when Trent came and we three sat together and talked for a time, Doug did not have any marked success, though his questions were put skillfully and very casually. Trent was immaculate in gray flannels, though he looked as if he had not slept well, and his inquiries after Mark, Juliet, and Madeline, who was still sleeping, were propriety itself. Walter we could see sunk moodily in a chair on the side porch, and Douglas said that Page was in the library.

"Not a very happy house party," I said with a wry smile.

"No," Trent agreed. "I'm sure she never thought— It looks as if we were in for another hot day."

"Sundays have a disagreeable habit of being hot," said Douglas absently. "Mr. Trent, I know that you'll think I'm curious, but the matter concerned me and I can't help wondering. Surely at some time Miss King gave you at least a hint of what changes she was going to make in her will?"

"I had no reason to suppose that she was going to change the existing one," said Trent.

"But she was; she worked on the new draft Friday night. We know that. And I can't help thinking that if we knew what the changes were—

"Possibly, but I doubt if they were anything drastic. Perhaps a little more care was to be taken in securing her heirs an assured income. I know she felt they were all inclined to be rather extravagant."

"Then there was no talk of cutting Walter out?"

"Not at all—" Trent flushed, as if he had betrayed himself. "I have no reason to believe so," he amended his statement quickly. "I was her friend, not her legal adviser."

I could not help smiling a little at Douglas, but he went on, undaunted. "Another thing puzzled me. When I looked over her papers there was not a scrap of personal correspondence. Perhaps it was burned with the new will, but if so, I wonder why?"

"Whoever burned the will that you speak of would probably take everything and not have time to look through the lot," said Trent politely.

"That's what we thought. But still, one would expect to find at least a few bits of personal matter when she had lived here for so long."

"Ellen was—not like other people," said Trent stiffly. "She did not write a great deal or receive any letters."

"I know. It was wonderful that she could write at all." Doug gave up, considering that courtesy did not permit him to go farther, I suppose. Presently murmuring something about cigarettes, he left us, and we chatted on about indifferent matters, until Walter put his head in at the open window and said curtly:

"Can you give me a minute, Trent?"

I thought at first Trent would refuse, but he went to the window and they talked for a few minutes, as again I was employed in the capacity of half unwilling listener. Walter's voice was low at first; then I heard:

"Sorry, but you've got to help me out, Trent. It's necessary, and the only way it can be done under the circumstances.

It won't put you in any danger, and I—" His voice became inaudible again, but I heard Trent.

"If you insist, I suppose I shall have to, but you're making a bad mistake and not helping yourself at all."

"Let me be the judge of that," said Walter rudely. "It needn't make you any trouble. Send—"

I heard no more until Trent said: "Very well, we'll arrange it that way."

"Thanks, I thought you'd see reason," said Walter, going back to the porch. Before Trent could resume his chair, Juliet came in.

"It isn't good for you to sit around like this," she said. "Come into the garden with me. It's lovely there, and I'll pick both of you a buttonhole posy."

Afterward she said that she despised herself for her duplicity, but we went gladly, and before we left the garden our footprints were neatly implanted in several spots of moist earth.

XII

Ellen's Diary

The little room that Ellen had called the "den" was the
only one in the house that I had never liked. It had only
one window and a large weeping willow grew outside that
so that it was always a little gloomy inside. Weeping wil-
lows are depressing trees anyway, and Ellen often talked of
cutting down this one, but never did.

The so-called library was misnamed as a matter of fact,
for there were book shelves on only one wall and for the
rest it was simply another living-room. The den was the
real library as well as having been old Mr. King's particular habitat. It seemed still to bear the impress of his char-
acter which, to judge by the room, had been a morose one.

The furniture was black walnut, good from a collector's
viewpoint, I imagine, but to me as depressing as the weeping willow. All the chairs were large and solid and steel en-
gravings on the walls failed to add cheer to the room. For
the rest, most of the walls were lined with heavy old books
in dark, ugly bindings. Ellen had a great deal of taste and
natural skill in home furnishing, and I always thought it a
proof of the force of her father's personality that she did
not change this room.

One virtue the place did have, however, and that was
coolness. Besides, it was not so popular as the other rooms
and we were all in such a state of nervous irritability and

dread that we rather tended to break into groups. It was hot after an early luncheon, with that peculiar and almost oppressive quiet that seems to belong to Sundays overlying the general restlessness of the household.

Walter was still on the side porch, smoking nervously, and Jack and Madeline, who had come down to lunch still a little pale, were in the library. White was taking a nap in the living-room, where Douglas was going over and docketing papers. I went upstairs, but it was smothering so near the roof and I could hear Mark moaning faintly, though his door was closed until Miss Barnes came out and set it ajar.

"It's rather stuffy and he needs air. I do wish he was able to be moved," she said. "But the doctor says no."

"Is he worse?" I asked, listening to the faint sounds from inside the room.

"He isn't resting so well. He's not conscious at all, you know. He may never be. I wish," said Miss Barnes with a little asperity, "that you'd tell Mr. White that. He keeps asking me if Mr. King has said anything coherent. He hasn't and he isn't likely to. I know it's important to let him know, but it's more important to me to save the boy's life."

"Certainly I'll tell him," I promised. "Don't you get any rest?"

"Yes, Miss Armstrong will be here any minute, and Miss Selby said that I could lie down in her room. I'll sleep until nine or ten o'clock."

She went back to Mark and I went downstairs, thinking of the den as a possible quiet and fairly cool refuge. Juliet was there before me and welcomed me with a smile.

"Come in. No, I'm glad to have company," she said. "This room gets on my nerves. I hate black walnut. No wonder Ellen's father was grouchy if he spent much of his time in here."

"How do you know he was—or did?" I said.

"Oh, Ellen said so once—she didn't say grouchy, of course. She used a nicer term—melancholy, I think. Did you know him, Uncle Gilbert?"

"I never even saw him, my dear. I didn't visit here until quite a while after he was dead—ten years, I suppose. Isn't Jackson around?"

"He was, but he's off somewhere now, probably digging up fresh evidence against Walter or trying to," said Juliet. "Like as not he is trying to follow the course that Walter took yesterday and discover more footprints."

She yawned.

"Thank Heaven for bright daylight, Uncle Gilbert. It makes night seem unreal. I wish it was, yet I've always been fond of night before. Do you know, I have a most unmaidenly wish that Doug and I were married—had been for some time—so I could have him near me tonight. It must be very comforting. Are you shocked?"

"It's too bad to disappoint you, Julie, but I'm afraid you young people don't shock people of my age half so easily as you like to think."

"I suppose not," said Juliet thoughtfully. "It's the fair fats and forties that are always raising their hands and eyebrows. Wake me if I snore."

I turned to the magazine I had carried with me, but Juliet did not sleep after all. After several moments of silence she got up and began to examine the rows of books.

"What things to have for surroundings," she commented. "Half of them seem to be bound abstracts and law books. Here are some atlases and a lot of old pictorial weeklies and geographical magazines. Travel must have been a hobby of his."

She pulled one out, a dusty old volume, and pored over it for a while.

"I was just thinking that I can travel now, if I want to. But it makes me feel rather sick to remember why. I suppose six per cent. bonds would be much more sensible."

She hoisted the heavy book back into place and went on with her scrutiny of the shelves.

"Look, Uncle Gilbert, here's a whole stack of French classics. What an odd mixture."

"Those probably belonged to Ellen's mother," I said. "I believe she was half French."

Juliet thumbed one over rapidly. "Queer old-fashioned print, and I've forgotten all I ever knew, which was never much."

"My dear," I said, "what about that nap?"

"You mean you want me to be still so you can read?" Juliet declared.

"No, but I hate to see you so restless."

"I know, Uncle Gilbert—I can't help it."

In turning to speak to me she knocked several of the dingy little volumes to the floor.

"See—I'm even turning clumsy."

In the act of replacing the books she stopped.

"Here's another one, tucked behind these. It's, why it's Ellen's diary, Uncle Gilbert. See, it has her name written on it."

I took the chunky leather book with its clasped covers into my hands. The name was written on the cover in a flowing hand very unlike the stilted precise writing of Ellen's later years. "'May 1901.' That was when she was about eighteen," I said. "Several years before I met her. The last entry is in 1909."

"That was when she lost her sight," said Juliet softly. "See how unsteady the last writing is. Uncle Gilbert, I feel terrible to ask it at all, but do we dare read this?"

"Under ordinary circumstances—"

"Under ordinary circumstances I wouldn't even ask. But there might be something hidden there—"

"That's the difficulty. There *might* be," I said. "But if there isn't, we've done a very unkind thing for nothing."

"But how can we know unless we look? If we don't, we may be letting something go by that would help us."

"Whatever you think," I said. "I'll leave it to you."

Juliet looked at the book for an instant longer, then she put it on the table and opened it resolutely.

"Ellen must know it isn't idle curiosity, and I'll skip all I dare to."

The first entries were written in a girlish vein that was hard for me to reconcile with the Ellen I had known; and made me feel that we were mere acquaintances, after all. There was mention of dances and parties and the name "Edward" recurred, frequently. He was then at college and she had received a letter from him, or been down to a prom or a football game.

The name of her younger sister, Rose, was there, too, and a "Philip" whom I could not at first place until a line which read:

> Philip had a quarrel with father today about his extravagance. He *will* not keep in his allowance, and the poor boy is so impulsive and hot-tempered. Father says he is not to be trusted with money, but I managed to patch things up between them, and they are good friends again. Father is apt to be easily vexed these days, but as I told Phil, he still misses mother dreadfully and we should try not to worry him.

"I didn't know Ellen had a brother," said Juliet, looking up at me. "Did you?"

"I remember now, but I had quite forgotten it. I think he died—or something else happened. Perhaps we shall find it, or I'll remember."

There was little of interest, except as an intimate human document is interesting, for a number of pages. Those pages covered a number of years, for Ellen, like most diarist starting with good intentions, did not write at all regularly. It was, for the most part, a happy record, though there were constant echoes of the responsibility she felt for her younger brother and sister. Rose was:

> So pretty, but rather frail and will not take good care of herself. She is a conscienceless coquette, too, but only laughs when I scold her and says that men's hearts will stand a lot of breaking.

Philip was apparently a rather lovable scapegrace, who was always needing money or in difficulties of some sort. Then came the entry in which King's second marriage was spoken of, with a little natural resentment which she tried hard to repress.

> She is very young and pretty, and rather silly, too. I don't see how father— But I ought not to say that and it is his right to marry again if he wishes. He is very lonely and she is bright and gay, but I did hope he would choose someone who would have more influence over Philip and Rose than I. They are both to go away to school, and I don't think I will stay here. Father is willing for me to spend a winter in town where I can attend lectures or even take up a special course or two at the university. I think he wants me to go away because Edward may come back here to go into business. I don't know what he has against Edward; he will never admit to anything, but

he says I should see a few more men before I
choose.

In the city, the record continued,

I met Gilbert Haynes today, through his sister
Margaret. He is very good looking and I think
we are going to be good friends, but I do not
think there is any danger of us falling in love.

"You see, my dear," I said, meeting Juliet's glance, "hard
as it is to believe, there it is."

"If you mean about your being good looking, it isn't at
all hard to believe," said Juliet with affectionate flattery.
"You still are." And tactfully she pretended that she had
skipped or failed to notice the next line:

Besides, he is in love with the prettiest little
dark-eyed thing, who does not half appreciate
him. I am afraid she will throw him over if
anyone very rich presents himself, and I am
sure she will regret it sometime in her life.

I am not unkind enough to hope so, but I wonder if
you did, Sylvia.

In general the accounts of her winter in the city were
brief and scattered. The last one told that Edward Trent
had come to see her and had asked her to marry him.

I do not want to marry against father's wishes, but I hope that now that he has new interests, he will not mind. I am going home next
month and we will talk to him then.

But almost at once, two days afterward, it was:

A telegram called me home last night, just before Pauline died. Poor little thing, her vitali-
ty was exhausted and she slipped away quietly
in spite of all the doctors could do. The baby
is alive and they think it will live, though it
is very delicate. Poor father seems stunned,
and I must stay and take care of him, and the
baby. Edward agrees with me that it would
not be right for me to think of leaving father
for several months, and we will not worry him
until he is much better and things are running with perfect smoothness here.

There were three or four brief entries speaking of the
baby's health and her father's continued depression. Of his
actual death there was no real account, only:

It is all over and everyone has been very
kind and I do not think they have talked
much, even in the village. 'Accidental death',
the doctor said, and he did not make us go
through the ordeal of an inquest. It might
very well have been an accident. Doctor Perry
prescribed those sleeping tablets himself, and
father might have ventured to take one or two
over the dose without knowing that his heart
was weak. But I know, of course, that there
was nothing accidental about it. I should have
guessed what he meant to do when he talked
to me yesterday, but I was so stunned by what
he said that I could think of nothing else.
    It is no wonder that father has always been
grim and taciturn, having to carry that secret
with him, and fearing that someday someone
would come who knew and shatter all our

pride and security. We have been proud—the Kings of Hillside—and now I find that our pride has been built on a false foundation and any day may humble us. Now it is for me to keep it hidden; we have gone too far to turn back. I hope I shall never have to tell the others; it is dangerous to share a secret with too many. I do not dare even put it down here, though it sometimes seems that I must confide in someone.

Phil and Rose are here and the funeral is tomorrow. It will be very quiet and then perhaps I shall find time to think.

The writing continued with only a space for the next day's date.

Father has left everything to me to administer. Rose and Phil are to have stated allowances, rather small, and I am to pay them. I had never thought of such a thing. Rose took it very well, but Phil is quite wild and said bitter things to me and threatened to bring the will into court. I told him that I would give him more, that things would be shared equally, but he said that he wanted independence, not doles handed out by an older sister. He would not talk any more and has gone out now, I hope to walk it off, but I am afraid to drink more than he should.

"I would like to see a picture of Philip," said Juliet. "I imagine he was a great deal like Walter. But he didn't come back—" Her forefinger indicated the next line:

Philip has disappeared. Beyond the night city train we have not been able to trace him. He is not with any of his friends. I hope and pray that he will come soon, sick and sorry, but I cannot help remembering how he flung back at me as he left the room, "You'll always be sorry for this, Ellen."

I am so tired and Rose is restless and the baby has not been well. I have been having such fearful headaches that it is hard for me to manage things and I must find time to go to a doctor, soon. I think I need glasses.

"Poor thing," said Juliet softly. "Oh, poor thing. It wasn't right, Uncle Gilbert!"

"It never is," I said. "See, there are very few entries and they are all very short." We read, down them silently.

May 20. Philip has never come back; never written.

May 22. I went to the doctor today and he advised me to go to the city to a specialist. He thinks it is my eyes.

May 26. I was to go into town today, but I have not been able to. Rose has married Robert West without the slightest warning to me. She slipped away Wednesday and wired me when they were married, and just before they sailed for France, too late for me to go to them. I can only pray that Robert West will never regret being connected with our family, and I have hope that he will not. After all, there is a good chance that nothing will ever come of it, and I am the only one who knows.

But I would have told him, if they had not
been so hasty.

May 31. I am going to be blind.

Juliet closed the book and she crying silently. "I almost
wish I hadn't read it," she said in a small voice.

"Though we have found something to think about,
haven't we?" said I. "And because we have gone this far, I
think we had better read that last entry. It won't hurt more
than the other has."

The writing was very wavering and there was a folded
browned paper between the last two leaves of the book.

August 14. While I can still see a little, I am
going to write this. It will make no difference
in the end; possibly a day more or less. If
I should die suddenly, which is not a likely
thing, I am leaving things to chance. If I
should ever be in danger of passing on and
I had decided by then that someone should
know I will try to tell someone or leave a
paper of some sort. The second would no
doubt be safer; simple communication left to
be opened in case of my death. Yet I do not
want to do even that just now. And in spite of
everything, I am going to be happy.

That was all. The letter bore the heading of a well-
known firm of private detectives.

My dear Miss King
We have done all that is possible to locate
your brother, but our best efforts have failed.
We traced him to a waterside saloon, where

he went one night but he was not seen afterward. You ask us to be quite frank. This place has a most unsavory reputation, and he was wearing some good jewelry and carrying a fair amount of money. It may be coincidence that a body was discovered in the river several days afterward, which in build and clothing would resemble your brother. Identification was impossible because of the state of the face and head. If you wish us to continue in this search, please let us know.

XIII

Walter Refuses to Answer

We had been nearly two hours over that small brown book. Now Juliet put it back on the shelves in the old position and placed the concealing books before it. Coming back, she sat on the arm of my chair and sank her pointed chin in her hands.

"Well, we've learned something," she said. "I wonder how much of it is going to help us."

"At present I don't see that any of it will," I said a trifle pettishly, being haunted by certain sentences in that unhappy record.

"Don't you? On the surface, I suppose it doesn't seem so," Juliet agreed. "But I am sure that there must be something there that will help us in the end."

She was proved right in time, but then I chose to say discouragingly:

"Whatever the skeleton in the King family closet, I can't just imagine how it could have any connection with Ellen's death."

"We don't know what it was that her father told her," said Juliet. "Have you any idea?"

"Well, let's try to be as commonplace as possible, so I won't suggest anything like the literal skeleton of some murdered enemy—"

Juliet frowned at my levity, which was certainly in bad taste, but I had just been dragged willy-nilly into the past and the trip had not agreed with me.

"I should guess at some crookedness in money matters that might have come to light some day," I suggested. "She spoke of their pride being built on a rotten foundation."

"Yes, that's reasonable. I thought of something along the same line," said Juliet. "Only it occurred to me—the influence of fiction, of course—that her father might even have been sent to prison. That would be a real blot on the 'scutcheon."

"The only difficulty with that is that I have the impression that the Kings have always been here. In that case, such a thing couldn't be hidden. We can find out easily enough, however."

"And Ellen's brother. I don't like that," said Juliet with a whimsical smile. "It runs too true to fiction again. The long-lost brother who returns, you know."

"But we don't know that he has returned," I objected, being of a literal mind.

"I have no idea that he has," said Juliet. "Very likely that was he who died so long ago. But if I hear of any stranger about this neighborhood—"

"You will investigate," I finished. "Well, we have not touched on one interesting thing—"

"Whether she did tell someone finally or leave some letter? No, but I've been thinking about it all the time, and if I did know that she left some record, and where to find it, I wouldn't know if it was right to read it."

"Yes, there's that to be considered with us," I said. "If Ellen kept that secret all these years—"

"We wouldn't want to undo her work? No," said Juliet, "that's it. None of us would tell, but it wouldn't be the same. And yet—oh, dear, if we only knew."

"Of course," I said cheerfully, "there's not too much use worrying over it. It's more than likely that she didn't tell and left no communication of any sort. If she did tell, Trent was her most likely confidant, and we'll never get it out of him. If she did leave a letter and kept it in her desk, it was burned that night along with the rest of the papers."

"Yes, though I can't believe she would keep a thing as important to her as that in a place so easy for anyone to get at," said Juliet. "It's more likely that she had a special place for anything of that kind."

"A safe deposit box would have been the best hiding place, but you might tackle Myra again," I said. "And I wish you more success with her than anyone has had so far."

"In the meantime—"

"In the meantime," I said firmly, "I am going to take a nap."

"If you can sleep on that shiny black thing masquerading as a couch, you are welcome to it," said Juliet. "I am going to talk to Doug."

As Juliet said, that slippery black couch was not conducive to comfort, but I managed to get in half an hour or so of sleep. I woke from an uneasy dream to find Myra standing over me with a certain grim look of amusement. I suppose an elderly man sleeping in a wilted collar and probably with his mouth open is not a dignified spectacle. I was decidedly cross as I struggled up, which impressed Myra not at all.

"I brought you in some lemonade and cakes," she said, putting a pitcher and plate of cakes on the table. "Lunch was early and dinner's going to be late—again. That shiftless Annie is lying down, still howling about her nerves. She wants to leave if the sheriff will let her, and if you ask me, she might as well. She won't get within ten feet of the cellar steps and she jumps a foot when she hears any noise. She spilled a whole plate of eggs that way this morning."

"But how will you manage if she does go?" I said.

"Oh, I'll get on all right. I've cooked for more than this amount of people before," said Myra. "It'll be just as well. Her eternal wailin' gets on my nerves. But she always was a slack-twisted creature, though she cooks good enough."

Juliet appeared at the door with Douglas behind her. "We came in to share your lemonade," she said, helping herself generously. "M-mm, that's good. Myra, will you please tell me something?"

Myra eyed her grimly. "Miss Juliet, I've always been fond of you, and I guess you know it, but don't count on me telling anything I think I'd better not, for all your coaxing."

"I know you won't tell unless you want to," said Juliet "But I can ask, can't I? How long have the Kings been here?"

"The fam'ly, you mean?" Myra looked at Juliet sharply, as if trying to guess the reason for the question. "Well, Mr. King's father built this house. I don't know just when, but I have kind of a remembrance hearing that it was when he was a small boy. Miss Ellen's father, I mean."

"And he always lived here?"

"All but for about five years when he was a young man. He went off to Europe and stayed a long time and come back married to this French girl he'd met over there. That is, she was half French, anyway." Juliet's eyes met mine triumphantly. "And they was away a year before Mrs. King died," Myra finished. "She was in bad health, poor lady, and they went back to France to see if it would help her, but it didn't and she died over there."

"Myra, did Ellen ever have a habit of keeping important papers in any special place?" Juliet's question was abrupt and Myra started.

"What papers? What place?" she said finally. "Miss Juliet, I think you need some sleep. You know Miss Ellen was particular about everything being just so."

"That wouldn't keep her from having a place for something valuable that she wanted to keep safe," said Juliet.

"I don't know anything about that! She kep' her law papers in a safe deposit box, and I don't know what else she would have or what you're talking about but I do know there ain't no secret drawers or things like that around here," said Myra scornfully. "And she wouldn't have used them if there had been."

"All right, Myra. I know it sounds foolish," said Juliet, with her most charming smile. "Perhaps I do need some sleep."

"I guess we all of us need that," said Myra grimly. "That nurse woman is getting hers right now. Someone come to relieve her—flyaway little creature that don't look like she knew her business. Doctor'll be back about nine to get her."

She went out, almost bumping into White at the door. He helped himself to the scraps of cakes remaining on the plate but refused Juliet's offer of lemonade.

"Feel like I needed something stronger," he said. He had the heavy-eyed, dull look of a man who has slept too long on a hot day. "But Jackson's out running around in this heat, so I shouldn't complain. I thought I'd better let him go and get some sleep if I'm going to watch tonight."

"I'll help out—if you trust me," said Douglas, probably remembering White's early morning nap in the hall.

"Oh, I trust *you*, all right," said White gloomily. "But I'm going to tell you something. The inquest is called for tomorrow, you see, in the morning, so they can have the—er—funeral in the afternoon. Well, I wouldn't be a bit surprised if they didn't return a verdict against King— Now, wait a minute. I don't want it, but Jackson's bound the evidence points that way, which it does, and he wants it

brought out at the inquest. Grimley agrees with him, and
if it is—like as not the jury will think like they do."

"But just what do you have against him?" said Doug.

White checked on his fingers.

"First, motive—the need of money and admitted quarrels with Miss King about it. He also admits that she said
he had to straighten up if he expected her to go on giving
it to him, and her letter to him proves that, anyway. That
when we know she was altering her will, is naturally going
to give rise at once to the idea that the change wouldn't
have been in his favor."

"Ideas aren't facts," said Juliet.

"No, but the jury is going to be people," said White
sensibly. "And people get ideas. Well, second is opportunity—that connecting door, unlatched on her side, the key
hidden in his room. He says that he did it because he was
foolish and thought it might implicate him. That might be
true and still not look very good for him. He admits that
he was in her room that night and we know he was, and we
have only his word for what time he was there. Of course,
we thought at first that she was shot from outside the window, but it would have done just as well for someone to
walk around there—someone she knew. The gun was probably his. I don't think that's of any great importance, since
everyone had access to it, but it will tell in the minds of
the jury, especially as someone took it out of the table and
it might have been him only he isn't admitting it."

"I suppose the other thing is that he was unaccounted
for at the time Annie heard someone in the cellar?" said
Douglas. "But so was Page and Myra—for that matter, so
were Juliet and Mr. Haynes, here, except on their own word
that they were in their rooms. And that goes for Miss West."

"Of course, but he had much the best chance of slipping in and out, and absolutely no verification of where
he was at the time," said White. "And last of all, unless he

changes a good deal, his own manner will be against him more than anything else with the jury, He's too flip and he sounds almost cold-blooded at times. Like when he said that he wouldn't have missed the first shot. Well, I want you, Martin, to tell him just what I've told you. Let him see what he's up against and if you've any influence at all, use it to make him sober down and be at least reasonably polite and serious when they're questioning him."

"I'll try," said Doug. "But I doubt if my influence is very great."

"Maybe not, but he's no fool, and don't hesitate to put it to him strongly that he's in a dangerous position. And if he knows anything that will help him out of it, tell him for God's sake not to try to keep it back."

"I'll try that, too," Douglas promised. "But that's more hopeless than the first."

"Do you really believe that he isn't—guilty?" said White curiously. "Would you defend him?"

"I'm a lawyer," said Doug. "And I'd defend him. As to being sure he isn't pretty well mixed up in this thing in some way, that's another matter."

"Well, I have an idea you'd put up a good fight for him," said White. "In a way, I'd be glad to bring matters to a showdown. We aren't getting anywhere and you folks are tired of staying here. Perhaps after tomorrow another day will see you free to go. What time is?"

"Nearly half past six," said Juliet. "I suppose we had better be freshening up for dinner, though Myra said it would be late, but Miss Barnes is in my room and I don't want to wake her."

"Well, there are only two bathrooms and I want a cold shower, so I think I'll go on now," said Doug. He stopped at the door, however, to let Miss Barnes come into the room, rustling in her stiffly starched white, and then waited with the rest of us to hear what she had to say.

"I remembered what you asked me to do, Mr. White," she began, taking a small slip of paper from one pocket. "So when my patient began to talk a little today, I took down what he said, as you told me to. I'm afraid it doesn't make a great deal of sense. He kept repeating, 'What are you burning?' in a perfectly expressionless voice; then he would mumble the last word, 'burning, burning, burning' over and over. That was the fever, I imagine. He mutters people's names, which is very natural. Then two or three times he has said 'Don't! Don't!' in a tone of terror. Those are really the only coherent words that he has said. I hope," she added, "that we can move him tomorrow to the hospital. It will probably either be that or he will be worse."

"If he does recover, do you think he will be perfectly— all right?" I said.

There was no doubt, of course, in any of our minds, what was the significance of Mark's few words.

"That depends. Doctor Grimley is doubtful."

Miss Barnes rained a number of technical terms on our defenseless and uncomprehending heads, but we managed to gather that there was some danger that Mark's injuries would affect his brain permanently. In any case, it would be weeks before he could be questioned at all.

"Well," said White, when she was gone, "at least what he said only agrees with what we supposed to be true. He stumbled on the burning of those papers—"

"Probably the only words he had a chance to say then were the ones that he mutters now," said Douglas rather grimly. "Well, I'll go on—" But again his cold shower was postponed as Jackson came into the room.

"Where's King?" he demanded. "I can't find him any-where around."

"He's been on the porch all afternoon," said White. "He was there when I came in here. Why do you want him?"

"I don't want him for anything in particular," said Jackson. He was hot and tired and very dusty. "But I want to be sure he's around. I'm not taking any chances, so I just looked around. Miss West and Page were in the sitting room and they said he came through there about fifteen minutes ago. Like as not he's made a getaway."

"Nonsense, said White. "He's probably upstairs."

"If he went up there, he isn't there now," said Jackson, wiping his face with a handkerchief which to judge from its appearance must have been used frequently for that purpose during the day.

"Well, it doesn't seem so important," White began placatingly.

"Maybe it isn't, unless he doesn't come back at all," Jackson snapped. "I want to know where he is, that's all."

"Oh well, if you feel that way about it, we'll look the house over again," said White, rising to go with him.

"We'll do that, all right, and more if necessary, but he wasn't here when I came into this room," Jackson said. "Like as not he's taking another of those little strolls like he did yesterday."

Their march through the house struck me a little comic, White being faintly resigned and Jackson almost militant. When they reached the kitchen Myra set the latter's fears at rest instantly. "If it's Mr. Walter you're looking for, he just came in through here and went upstairs the back way. No, I don't know what he was doing, and I don't care."

Walter himself descended the front stairs into the hall before Jackson had started up after him.

"I was in my room," he said in answer to the constable's brusque question.

"I don't mean just now. You weren't in your room fifteen minutes ago, because I looked to see."

"My God, but that's privacy for you," said Walter. "Suppose I was taking a bath—"

"You weren't—I looked there, too," said Jackson. "You weren't anywhere about the house or in the gardens."

"You wanted to see me?" said Walter in that indefinably insolent way of his.

"I wanted to know where everyone was. It's up to me to see that none of you skip out till you're free to go." Jackson was hot and exasperated, and in such circumstances he was not inclined to be tactful. "There's an inquest tomorrow and none of you are free to come and go, you least of all. Where were you?"

"I stepped out for a breath of fresh air," said Walter blandly. "You can probably find my tracks if you look for them; and I don't think that you'll find that I've been interring any slain victims in the woods."

He passed on into the living room, and White looked at Douglas with a despairing headshake.

"What can you do with a fellow like that? For heaven's sake, talk to him like a Dutch uncle, Martin."

XIV

The Substituted Fever Powders

We all sat around in the living room while we waited for Myra to announce dinner, too dispirited from the heat and the general situation to make even our customary pretense of polite conversation. The two girls were pale, but Madeline's pallor was really ghastly, and the small strip of courtplaster over the cut on her cheek looked like a dark scar. Page kept glancing at her concernedly, and murmuring solicitous questions. I find that I have rather neglected Page; we all inclined to overlook him, and we should not have done so.

While we were sitting, with Jackson by the window looking like a truculent watchdog, Trent's car stopped in front of the house and he came in with a package that the doctor had sent to Miss Barnes.

"I'll take it to her," Walter volunteered.

This would have been surprising, except that by his glance at him it was done in direct defiance of Jackson. For an instant Jackson appeared on the point of forbidding him to go, but he did not, and Walter went and returned almost immediately.

"Have you had dinner yet, Uncle Edward?" said Madeline. We all inclined to welcome Trent unduly, simply because he represented a certain distraction coming from the outside.

Trent smiled.

"No, and I'm not likely to have it at all, unless I go back to the village or fry myself some bacon and eggs. Mamie took this time to ask for a vacation and I gave it to her."

"Is that your cook?" said Jackson, turning from his window.

"Yes. She's a very good cook," said Trent gently. "But inclined to be talkative."

I avoided meeting Juliet's delightful smile.

"When things are—over, here, I may go away for some time, so I didn't object to her lay off, as she called it."

"Then you must stay and have dinner with us," Madeline said. "Myra is doing the cooking, but whatever we have will be better than burned bacon and eggs."

"I'm too good a camp cook to burn my bacon and eggs," Trent said. "Besides, Myra has too many now."

But Madeline insisted that he stay, and in the end he did—not too unwillingly, I thought. When we went out to dinner, I was last, with Juliet and Douglas. Jackson had made some pretense to join Madeline and was saying: "You didn't tell me that Trent was your uncle."

"Certainly I didn't. He isn't my uncle," said Madeline. "I called him Uncle Edward when I was a child. I knew him from the time I first came here."

"I see. I know he and your aunt were great friends. Did they ever quarrel—I mean, disagree, about anything?"

"They did not!" said Madeline with a sudden flush of color. "Never! They were always the best of friends and I think your question is quite out of place!"

"Jackson is certainly not making himself popular tonight," Doug remarked in a low voice, as Madeline left the constable abruptly and took a seat at the table as far removed from him as possible.

"The poor man is only doing his duty," said Juliet. "And at that, he's far from being a fool. I wonder—"

"What?" I said.

"Nothing. I'll tell you later."

"I wonder what he would think if he knew—well, what we do," she explained, when after dinner we three were on the side porch together. "I doubt if he would be greatly enthused, though. He has a very practical mind."

"Probably he'd start combing the Rogues' Gallery for pictures of old Mr. King," said Doug.

"Very likely. What about Ellen's safe deposit box?" I asked. "It struck me that we might be overlooking a good bet there."

Douglas shook his head.

"No. As I told Juliet, I'm perfectly familiar with the contents of the box, and there is nothing but a few legal papers and some securities in it. No documents of any other kind. I hate to disturb you, Juliet," he added presently. "But in a few minutes will you go back into the living room, and when you go by Walter tell him to come out here. I promised White I'd talk to him and we might as well get it over."

"I'll go," I offered, a little too eagerly.

Doug grinned.

"No, you don't. I want you right here. Walter has some respect for you and you can back me up in what I say."

Doug, when Walter came, was very tactful and as brief as possible, but he did not hesitate to put it to him "strongly" as White had advised. To my relief, Walter took it very quietly, without an interruption.

"So that's the way it stands," he said, with a mirthless smile, when Doug was through. "I hadn't let myself realize there was so much against me. It's good of you to tell me."

"And you'll do your best not to antagonize the jury?" I put in.

"I suppose I'll try, but I never get very far with any good resolutions I make to curb my tongue. No, he's right," said

Walter. "It looks pretty bad for me, but I'll have to struggle through it the best way I can."

"There isn't anything—" Doug began. "That is, don't you know anything that might help you out?"

"Short of someone discovering—who did it, there's nothing that can help me," said Walter moodily.

"Well, if they do return a verdict of guilty against you at the inquest, that doesn't mean you're condemned," said Doug cheerfully. "I could put up a good fight for you myself, and with a cracker jack criminal lawyer you'd have a good deal more than a fighting chance."

"You think that?" said Walter, his face lighting up momentarily. "Would you defend me?"

"Yes, I think I would, if you wanted it," said Doug. "But you'd be better off with someone of more experience than I have in that line."

"No, if I have to fight for it, I'll take my chances with you," said Walter. "Well, tomorrow does it. Page won't be sorry if it turns out that way."

"Why should I feel sorry for him?" said Doug, looking after him as he went back into the living room. "On the face of things, I'm a fool to say that I'll defend him, though they can't prove exclusive opportunity or motive."

"He never had much chance. His father was a rascal and his mother a fool," I said. "Poor combination."

I had overheard several, things not meant for my ears since the night before, and I was destined to hear one more supposedly private conversation before the day ended. In all cases, I have to confess that I listened without any strenuous effort to avoid eavesdropping.

I had gone to the front door about nine o'clock to see if Grimley was coming; at least, that was my excuse. It was really that the brightly lighted room and our cheerless company made me nervous and restless. Madeline and Walter were standing outside in the shadows. I could not see their faces plainly, but I thought Madeline had been crying.

"Do be careful—"

"I'm trying to," said Walter grimly. "But it's damn hard to do."

"I know, but a false step just now—"

"And I'm arrested," said Walter. "Don't think I haven't given it some consideration. I'll take my chances and count on getting through. The sooner we're out of here, the better."

"I know," said Madeline again. "It's not just that they're watching you; they might suspect any one of us."

"Not a chance. I'm elected to that honor, so don't worry about that."

"But I do. I'm fond of you, Walter—"

"Fond? Well, that will do, I suppose, and you'll probably have a chance to prove it."

I stepped back into the hall until I could see into the living room. Jackson had just stood up and was looking about him, frowning. I went back through the hall quietly and outside this time.

"I think our friend the constable will be strolling out here almost any time," I remarked casually. "He seems to be getting restless."

Walter took the hint, but he scowled and did not thank me as he went back into the house. Madeline moved over to my side.

"Mr. Haynes, do you really think that they'll bring in a verdict against Walter?"

"I don't know, my dear. White is afraid that they may. If he will just be careful what he says—"

"That's what I've been trying to tell him, but he's so reckless. Don't let Jack know that I've been talking to Walter, please. Jack is so jealous, and I suppose I've given him cause to be, but I've known Walter all my life, and when he's in trouble like this I can't avoid him even to please Jack."

"No, I should think not," I said. "He may not need your championship, but if he does, I'd tell Jack to—er—where to head in."

"He doesn't realize that we're all mixed up in this. I benefit more by Ellen's will than anyone else does, and it will be good to be independent," said Madeline. "Why, Jack himself benefits indirectly, but he was almost angry when I told him so, and said that that was no reason I shouldn't see how strongly everything pointed to Walter. Oh, I wish it was over."

"Another day and it probably will be," I said comfortingly. "We'll all feel better to be away from here."

"But we may be watched just the same, and I don't want to be," said Madeline childishly. "It makes me so nervous. It's time for the doctor to come, isn't it? Miss Barnes says that Mark is just the same. If he could speak do you suppose this would be ended?"

"We haven't any way of knowing that. Perhaps, but they doubt if he'll be normal for a long time, if ever." Jackson came outside, looking at us sharply, and Madeline, after a commonplace remark about the weather, left us. Jackson lighted a cigar and puffed at it savagely.

"This house gets on my nerves—be glad when this is over," he said surprisingly. I would not have credited him with having nerves. "That girl, now— Miss West," he went on after an instant. "Both those young fellows are crazy about her. If either of them had been the one to be killed, we wouldn't have so far to look. Not that we have as it is. Money seems the only motive for Miss King's death, and there's plenty of people benefiting."

"Yes, so Miss West just pointed out. She herself benefits more than anyone, and so does Page through her."

"Sure, and either of them could have done it. Well, no—not Miss West. She and Miss Selby have the only real alibis, and with them there's always a chance that they were in cahoots."

"Ridiculous," I said stiffly. "Juliet wouldn't—"

"Sure, she wouldn't," said Jackson amiably. "Neither would Miss West, though she would be the more likely of the two. Naturally you get riled at such suggestions, but it's my business to think of things like that."

"Am I under suspicion?" I asked. "I had as good an opportunity as anyone."

"Not you," said Jackson. "You couldn't have done it."

Perhaps I should have been flattered by this prompt avowal, but I wasn't. There was something vaguely belittling about it.

"You know," said Jackson, perhaps moved to confidence by the warm, starry night—or the influence of a good cigar. "There's something funny about those footprints in the garden—"

Miss Barnes' voice, calling imperatively, interrupted him.

"Mr. White! Mr. Jackson!"

She was standing at the head of the stairs, and it was plain that her professional calm was badly disturbed.

White came out into the hall, followed inevitably by the others.

"What is it; Miss Barnes? Has something happened?"

"Yes, something has, or might have. I'm not going out of sight of this room, and I want you to call the doctor and tell him to arrange to have my patient moved at once. I'm certain he can stand it, and it will be safer for him than being left here."

Her look swept us all with definite hostility.

"I don't understand you, nurse," said Jackson. "What do you mean—'safer'?"

"I mean that someone wants Mr. King out of the way, and if I hadn't had my eyes open, he might be dead now," said Miss Barnes. "If you come up here, I'll explain. I won't risk going away."

We went up, an obedient herd, filling the narrow hallway. The pretty little nurse, Miss Armstrong, was leaning against the wall, looking pale and frightened. I wondered what Miss Barnes had been saying to her—a great deal, I imagined.

"This is what happened," said Miss Barnes, holding out a small box, with some half dozen folded white packets in it such as various powders are often wrapped in. "These are for fever—that's as near as I need explain their use, I suppose. I have given Mr. King only one, but several minutes ago he seemed unusually restless and I decided to give him another. As soon as I took one out I knew that they were not the powders the doctor gave me."

"You tasted them?" said White.

"Tasted them? No, I didn't care to take the risk," said Miss Barnes scornfully. "I didn't need to, to know they are not the original ones. The paper in which they are wrapped is of a different kind from those the druggist here uses. I compared it with some of his that I have. But what first called my attention to the difference was that they are not folded in quite the same way that Mr. Young does. It is just a little difference, but it was enough to make me decide that something was wrong. Besides, there are seven here. I only had six, so someone was careless."

"You couldn't possibly be mistaken—"

"I could not, Mr. White," said the nurse briefly. "And since my attention was called to it, I was sure that someone had been at things on the table. We nurses are particular about arrangements like that, and there were several things—a glass, a spoon and so on, that I am sure had been disarranged a little. So I want to get this boy out of here."

"I'll phone," said White meekly.

"You left him alone several times?" said Jackson, as White started for the telephone in the lower hall.

"Twice—when I went to the kitchen to make broth and when I took it back. Miss Armstrong was on duty from two until seven, and she was out of the room—"

"Only twice," said Miss Armstrong defensively.

"It would only take an instant to substitute those powders," said Jackson. "I suppose it is fairly impossible to try to trace the whereabouts of everyone at those times, even if you remembered when you were gone from the room."

"I was in the kitchen for the first time while Myra was preparing dinner and practically everyone was upstairs," said Miss Barnes. "When I left—that is, when I came back here, I think they had gone downstairs."

"So that anyone—" Jackson did not finish his sentence. "Those powders were not in the package Mr. Trent brought you?"

"No. As to that package, I was not in the room when it was brought up," said Miss Barnes. "That was while I was still in the kitchen the first time."

"Oh—I see," said Jackson slowly.

Walter's face was expressionless, but you could see his jaw muscles tighten. That slow "I see" was like the snapping on of handcuffs in all our minds, though I remembered at once how quickly Walter had returned from his errand.

"Well," Jackson finished laconically, "everyone was up here for at least part of the time that you were away—except Mr. Trent."

"I'm afraid that I must join the rest in that category," said Trent. "You must remember that I came up to wash my hands just before dinner. Miss Barnes was coming upstairs again as I went down."

"Yes, that was the second time," said Miss Barnes. "Well, Mr. White?"

"We will arrange to send the ambulance at once," said White. He looked tired and depressed. "Perhaps—it is after nine—it would be better if you all went to bed and got some rest."

We obeyed his suggestion, which might as well have been a command. About half an hour we heard the grind of the ambulance as it stopped, and the voices of the stretcher bearers before the house settled down to stillness; and that night was very quiet.

XV

Another Murder

When I was a child I always liked to see my mother sew patchwork; a lap full of scraps of assorted shapes and colors growing into a definite pattern. It was mental patchwork I tried to do as I lay in bed that night, but the little scraps of surmise and knowledge refused to coalesce.

"A crazy-work quilt," I remember thinking before I went off to sleep at last.

I was evidently more exhausted than I knew, for there was no waking that night, and it was after eight o'clock when I sat up, blinking in the bright sunlight.

Doug was already dressed and combing his hair in front of the old-fashioned bureau.

"You'd better hustle," he said, grinning at me companionably. "Everyone must be late this morning, because Myra just sounded that warning gong. You were sleeping so beautifully that I hated to wake you up. Have a good night?"

"Fine, thanks," I said, beginning to tumble into my clothes. "First one since we came. I feel a hundred per cent. better. I take it there was no excitement last night?"

"Not a bit At least, I didn't hear anything, which wasn't too surprising as I slept like the dead. Jackson said he'd stay till around midnight and then White could guard. He probably had a nice little snooze himself," said Doug with another grin.

"Oh, well, I imagine there was nothing in particular to watch for, especially since Mark is out of the house. I wonder what the chances are that the nurse was mistaken?"

"I'd like to think she was, but I'm afraid not," said Doug, sitting on his tumbled bed while I finished dressing. "We should have expected something like that, you know. If Mark saw the person in the cellar that night, whoever it was is in danger if he recovers enough to tell what he knows."

"It would be the most simple way of learning the truth certainly, but it doesn't seem likely now that it will be the way. What about that diary of Ellen's and what it told us? Do we try to find out what it was her father told her?"

"I'm inclined to say yes, though I'm doubtful what bearing it has on the case, and I don't see exactly how we are going to succeed, anyway," said Doug. "But we can't afford to let anything slip by, and strange secrets have a habit of cropping up and causing trouble."

Everyone but Walter was downstairs by the time we got there, but breakfast was not on the table.

"Sleepy heads," said Juliet. "You should have been up hours ago. Myra is saying uncomplimentary things about you and Walter in the kitchen. Come see how lovely the garden looks this morning."

Juliet is not given to raptures over nature, and one of the things I like about her is that she never asks you to admire scenery audibly. So it was quite apparent that it was for some other reason that she wanted us to come to her at the open window.

"The roses are gorgeous, aren't they? I wish I knew their names— The book is gone from the Den," she said, without any change in the expression of her voice.

"Ellen's—"

"Yes. Act as if we were talking about the flowers. I thought about it all night, every time I was awake, and I decided that we didn't dare ignore it. There were some things I couldn't remember exactly, so I was up before anyone and went in there. I was going to copy one or two sentences. It was gone."

"You're sure?"

"Absolutely. I looked thoroughly and I'm quite sure— that those small pink roses are Cecile Breuners. Aren't they, Mr. White?"

"You're right. And the big yellow ones over there—"

Doug and I left White to his exposition of horticulture and strolled into the hall, leaving Madeline and Jack Page to their interminable tête-à-tête.

"Was anyone around when you were reading that?" said Douglas abruptly.

"Not a soul, that we saw. But our backs were to the door," I remembered. "And we were pretty well engrossed in what we were doing. Then there's that window. It would be easy for anyone to stand behind the leaves of that weeping willow without our noticing."

"Either someone did see you or someone knew that book was there and decided to remove it without knowing you had found it. At any rate, it isn't to be dismissed as lightly as I thought. When do we eat, Myra?"

Myra, appearing from the kitchen, folded her hands in her brown gingham apron and regarded us sourly.

"So *you're* up," she said. "We'll eat when you're all here."

"We are and starving to death," said Douglas.

"No, you ain't—that lazy Walter hasn't come down, and I'm not going up to wake him."

"Oh, that's right. Well, I'll go and get him down," said Doug. "Let the rest of them go ahead, Myra. He won't mind."

"What is it?" said White, joining us again, evidently having exhausted the beauties of the rose garden. "Young

King not up yet?" He paused for an instant. "That's—queer," he said slowly. "He must have waked up with the gong and all of us stirring around. We'd better have a look. If he's gone, Jackson will have plenty to say to me—"

They started up the stairs, but I remained where I was, saying to myself tritely that innocent men don't run away.

"Locked, of course." Doug's voice carried clearly, "King! Walter!"

I found myself half-way up the stairs and stopped, shivering with some unhappy premonition as I saw Douglas go into Page's room and knew that he was going to step through the window and onto the porch.

White and I waited. I was vaguely aware that the alarm had spread to those in the living-room and that they were crowding behind me onto the stairs. Then there was the sound of a sliding bolt, Walter's door opened and Doug came out.

"Is he gone?" said White.

"Not the way you mean, but he's gone," said Doug. "I think he's been dead for some time."

"You mean he's killed himself?"

It was Madeline's voice. Without waiting for his answer, she broke into wild crying. Juliet and Page took her back into the living-room and I came up the remaining steps, achieving each one, it seemed to me, by a distinct effort.

"I don't know if it's suicide," said Doug then. "It looks like it. The window was down and—I may be mistaken—but I think there's a faint odor of peach blossoms. He'd been drinking. You'd better not bother to come in," he said to me kindly.

I would have been glad to avail myself of his advice, but in itself it was enough to stiffen my pride and draw me in. Walter had been sitting by the table and there was a flat bottle of whisky and a half-filled glass within reach of his lifeless hand. His head had fallen forward on his arm and his face was hidden so that, except for the dreadful rigidity of his body, he looked as if he had fallen asleep. White touched one hand lightly.

"Stone cold," he said. "You're right, Martin—some time in the night, I suppose. He probably sat here and thought things out— Had he been drinking?"

"He always drank," I said. "And since Saturday, more than ever. I thought anyone would have noticed it."

"I did," Doug nodded. "He let up for a while yesterday. Look, sheriff, under his right hand."

"I shouldn't disturb anything until Grimley can get here," said White doubtfully. "But—"

He tugged gently at the edge of paper that showed. A pencil rolled toward the table's edge as he drew the paper free. There were only two words, "I know," and then the writing trailed off as if death had intervened.

"We'll have to get the contents of that glass analyzed," White said, looking at it, but not offering to touch it.

"I'd get the contents of the whole bottle analyzed if I were you," said Doug quietly.

"Of course—but what's wrong, Martin?"

"You think it's suicide?"

"Don't you?" White and I said almost together.

"No, I don't," said Doug curtly. "I think everything points the other way— to murder."

"But why?" said White. "He had reason to take the easiest way out of his difficulties. The room was locked—"

"We all locked our rooms last night," said Doug. "And I think Walter meant to stick it out." He pointed to the whisky bottle. "If you find poison in that, will it make you think differently?"

"A man doesn't put poison in an entire bottle of whisky when he only needs to drink a few swallows to die, if that's what you mean," said White. "Yes, that would make a difference. What else?"

"Where is the bottle, or box, that contained the poison?" said Doug. "We don't see it here."

"We might find it here, or outside. He may have thrown it from the porch," said White.

Almost against my wishes—I had hoped that this was the end and not just another ghastly step—I was forced to side with Doug.

"People committing suicide very seldom bother to hide the means. I'm not a detective or psychologist, but I've had enough experience with human nature to know that. The natural thing would be to pour out the poison and drink, without bothering to conceal the container first."

White's face was harassed.

"I had hoped that this was the end," he said, putting my own thoughts into words. "Perhaps not."

"And this writing," said Doug, motioning toward it. "A man about to drink poisoned whisky doesn't wait until he has drunk to write. He writes before. Walter King had some decent spots. I think if he had killed himself because he was guilty of Ellen's murder, he would have left some confession. Not just to clear things up, but most suicides do leave some explanation, particularly if they kill themselves for the reason he would have."

"This paper, then, would be an attempt to tell something he knew," said White. "But it's very likely he had begun to write, got that far and took his drink. He'd die too quickly to write anything after he had drunk. All right, you win, on the evidence at present. We'll lock things up and call Grimley."

Grimley came at once, with Jackson.

"We should have looked for something like this," the latter said disgustedly. "We should have watched—"

He was inclined to scoff when White put Doug's theories before him, but ended by shaking his head doubtfully.

"There's something in what he says, and we'll soon see. If he's right, it's simply more devilment and I was on the wrong track. Miss Barnes was right, those weren't the powders Grimley gave her."

"What were they?" said White.

"Haven't been able to have them properly analyzed yet, but Grimley says he thinks they are very strong sleeping powders and that in young King's condition one would have sent him off very nicely. He said that he thought the dose had been increased; that is, two doses had been put in one paper and then rewrapped."

"That seems to me pretty stupid," said Douglas. "The only stupid thing that's been done so far."

"Oh, I don't know. If the nurse in charge hadn't been pretty clever and darned careful, it might have slipped by easily enough and no one would have been wise to what had really happened. Those powders weren't put up here, we know that much," said Jackson. "And knowing it doesn't help us any. It will be almost impossible to trace them. They might have been bought in the city or any one of half a dozen towns near here."

Grimley called to White and he went upstairs, returning in a few minutes.

"Prussic acid," he said briefly. "It's up to us to get busy and see if we can trace it."

"It's not so easy to buy that stuff," said Jackson. "Ten chances to one, it wasn't bought, but come into possession of in some other way. What about the inquest?"

"We'll have to hold it—go through a few necessary motions, anyway," said White. "Grimley's going to arrange for that. Naturally they can't put off the funeral any longer. But these people will have to stay here."

"Yes, we still have plenty on our hands. I can't see much to be gained by asking questions here," said Jackson. "If there proves to be poison in all that bottle and it's not suicide, anyone could have poisoned it during the day. You say he always had liquor around?"

"I never knew him not to," said Douglas. "And it was unusually evident, this time, that he did have."

"There's always a chance of two unconnected murders," Jackson mused. "Bad blood between King and this fellow, Page. Where is everyone else, by the way?"

"Miss West has gone to her room and Miss Selby is with her," said White. "I left Page walking up and down the library worrying about her."

"There's no reason he should pretend to be sorry about King's death, I guess," said Jackson reasonably. "But I don't suppose he has any alibi—don't see how he could have; and he certainly wasted no love on King."

I did not speak; let Douglas tell of Jack's warning to Walter if he though it necessary. I did not.

"For that matter," Jackson finished, "neither did that old lady in the kitchen care a great deal about him."

"What were you starting to tell me last night about those footprints?" I said boldly.

Jackson looked at White rather guiltily.

"Oh, there's no harm in telling, I suppose. Trent's footprints were in the garden, all right, as nearly as we can be sure without taking casts. But I found some others just outside in the path and those weren't Trent's, and as nearly as I can check up, they don't resemble anyone's that we know, but I'd take my oath that they were made by old shoes."

"Probably a hobo," said Douglas prosaically.

Juliet came down the stairs slowly, nodding to Jackson before she said:

"Madeline is better, now, and she wanted me to tell you that she'll be ready for the inquest."

"All right, that's good," said White. "I'll see Grimley. We want to get these things over for you folks. You'll have to stay now until the second inquest is over. After that, I'm inclined to let you go."

He looked at Jackson.

"Sure, I should think that would, be all right," said Jackson surprisingly.

"I wonder what he has up his sleeve, now?" Doug muttered to me, but I could only shake my head.

The inquest was very brief, the mere formality that White had promised. The jury found themselves disappointed of a logical suspect as they brought in the time-worn verdict, "Murder by person or persons unknown." Early that afternoon Ellen was buried in the shady countryside graveyard, and those of us who were left went back to her home in the glaring dust of the afternoon.

XVI
More Questions and Answers

Juliet found me in the Den that afternoon, engaged in an occupation which no one involved in a mystery seems able to escape—the making of a list of unsolved questions.

"Just trying to pass the time away," I said somewhat sheepishly, as she drew my hand away from the paper and read over my shoulder:

1. What changes was Ellen going to make in her will?
2. What do Myra and Trent know—if anything?
3. Who was in the hall that second night and what was the reason for that performance?
4. Who was outside the house that same night?
5. Who did I hear going down the back stairway the night Ellen was killed?
6. Is there any significance to the scraps of paper that we found in the cellar?
7. What were Walter and Trent talking about yesterday?
8. What is the "family secret" to which Ellen refers? Has it any connection with the murders?

"Answer to number, one—we don't know," said Juliet checking the questions off on her fingers. "If we did— Two, and rather slangy, I'll make it my business to worm something out of Myra. Three and four—again we don't know. As to the reason for the tapping, I think Doug's idea that someone might have tried to scare a possible murderer is about as good as any. Suppose Myra thought Walter did it. She'd be quite capable of such a thing, and knocking Madeline down, too. She's awfully strong. Or Mr. Trent, as Doug suggested."

"How could he get in?"

"Well, there you are. How could he? Five, we don't know, either, and I never saw those scraps of paper."

"They seem to be from a letter, and we were inclined to think that they were taken to the cellar and burned because they happened to be with the other papers that were taken. I don't remember the exact wording of the phrases that were complete, but White kept the pieces and he'd probably show them to you."

"I'll ask him," said Juliet. "As to number seven, you've been keeping something to yourself, Uncle Gilbert, and you'd better out with it, if this is going to be a successful partnership."

"My dear, I seem fated to appear in the light of a snooping old gossip, and I'm not sure that it isn't the proper light," I said. "Walter asked Trent to do something for him, which he didn't want to do. Walter insisted on his help, and said it would be no danger for him."

"'Danger' was the word he used?"

"Yes, I'm sure of that. And Trent agreed finally, but I remember he said something about Walter doing himself no good to ask it."

"Um-m," said Juliet thoughtfully. "Suppose Walter knew more than we do about Mr. Trent, or that he was

trying to help himself out of the jam he was in? Do you
like Mr. Trent, Uncle Gilbert?"

"Very much. I always have," I said promptly. "If you're
thinking of him—"

"I like him, too, but we've got to consider everyone.
And he's known Ellen a long time," said Juliet. "He'd be
more apt to be—connected with the Kings' past history
than anyone but Myra. And that brings us to the last questions and to the first, I say I don't know, and to the second, yes, I'm sure it has. There's a ninth question, Uncle
Gilbert—who took the diary and why?"

"I can only give you a dose of your own medicine and
say 'we don't know.' If it was not someone who saw us,
Myra would be most apt to know where it was, and she
might take it simply to hide it from strangers," I said.
"But its taking wasn't a criminal act. I think anyone would
have a natural curiosity to know what we were so intent on
if they saw us."

I turned over the sheet of paper and wrote at the top
of it "motive" and "opportunity" and drew a line down
the paper between the two words. "Here's another way of
getting at it," I said.

Juliet took the paper from my hand and wrote her
own name first under "motive," following it with Doug's,
Madeline's, Myra's, Walter's, Jack's and Mark's.

"There's always an off chance that Walter did kill
Ellen," she said. "We don't know yet that it wasn't suicide.
But if he was murdered—"

She wrote Jack's name, then Myra's and put a question
mark after it, and then wrote Trent's in like fashion.

"Opportunity?" she said. "Anyone but Madeline and
myself. In the case of the poisoning, everyone. All of us
had access to that gun, too. We didn't know about it, of
course—I mean you and I and Doug didn't."

"Which doesn't get us very far," I said. "What's that for?" She had penciled a large black question mark after the heading "motive."

"Just a reflection of my own thoughts. The motive we're taking for granted is money, but it might be something else that we don't know about. Oh, well, let's tear the thing up and forget it," she said, with a sudden revulsion of feeling.

I did not destroy my work, but folded the paper and put it away in an inner pocket. Juliet was silent for perhaps five minutes, only to ask suddenly:

"Was she very pretty, Uncle Gilbert?"

"Who, my dear?" I said, though I knew quite well by her tone to whom she referred.

"The—the girl that you didn't marry. But it's horrid of me to ask. I'm stupid this afternoon."

"I don't mind in the least. She was very pretty, much prettier than you, but you have always reminded me of her. She was little and her hair was like yours, but she was all color—"

"Where I'm all drab. There, I've paid myself back," said Juliet. "But I think it was horrid of her not to marry you, Uncle Gilbert."

"Well, I thought so, myself," I said philosophically. "But I was struggling along in law and hating it, and no one guessed that my father would eventually leave me very well off. Besides, if they had, he was extremely healthy just then. Her mother wanted her to marry well—and she did."

"And was sorry for it, I'll bet," said Juliet. "I'm sure she must have been, whenever she saw you and then looked at her Mr. Armesby."

"There's not much you youngsters don't find out," I murmured. "I remember my sister, saying that it would take all his money to gild a pill like Armesby, but you mustn't think he always looked as he does now. But aside

from looks, I'm afraid Madge was right. I didn't see her,
though, so she couldn't compare us if she had wanted to."

"What do you think Doug will do if I don't marry him
some day?" said Juliet, with apparent irrelevance.

"Oh, when he is convinced that you are never going to
marry him—and it takes a good deal to convince Doug—
he will probably marry someone else some day," I said
heartlessly.

"That's just what I've been thinking, and I couldn't
stand that," said Juliet frankly. "I'm not just a dog in the
manger, either—and the worst of it is, I can't imagine ever
being married to anyone but Doug. I don't want to get
married at all, but I guess I'll have to, or risk losing him.
Isn't it terribly hot, Uncle Gilbert. I'm suffocating—"

As a matter of fact, it was quite comfortable in the house
that afternoon, but Doug's entrance called the long-suf-
fering weather into use for this sudden change of subject.

"I just had a 'phone call from Jackson," said Doug.
"He's down in the village and his car has gone blooey, so
he wants me to come down and get him."

"Why doesn't he hire one?" said Juliet.

"I'm sure I don't know. Maybe there's, none to hire at
that one-horse garage, or perhaps it's the desire for my
charming company that makes him ask me. At any rate,
I'm off in a minute or two," said Doug, sitting on the arm
of my chair. "I thought you'd like to know what else Jackson said. There was poison in all of that whisky."

"They analyzed it already?"

"It's very easy to do, sir—I could myself if I hadn't forgotten all my chemistry."

"So that knocks out the suicide idea," said Juliet, "Well,
none of us believed it, anyway. But why poison the whole
bottle when if it had been just in the glass we would have
been sure it was suicide?"

"I guess it was a case of have to," said Doug. "Couldn't very well wait around until Walter had decided to take a drink and then get it into the glass without his objecting. Whoever did it, knew his habits."

"That doesn't help much. All of us knew he drank," I said. "No fingerprints, I suppose?"

"It's a fingerprintless case, so far. Oh, Walter's were on the bottle and glass, of course. Jackson took them as a matter of form."

"Is that all you have to tell us?" said Juliet, as Doug continued to sit on my chair arm, frowning a little.

"No, not quite. I was debating whether to tell this, but since it's a partnership I'd better. Fact is," said Doug, flushing a little, "I've been doing some phoning to the city, prying into other people's business. I had a sort of hunch, call it that for want of a better name, and I phoned a friend of mine who's a broker and asked him if he knew how Page rated financially."

"Well?" said Juliet impatiently, as he paused.

"You know, he's supposed to well off, aside from his salary. But Broderick told me that Page had been speculating, not wisely but too well, the result being that he's pretty well cleaned out."

"They will do it," I remarked. "Every young broker or insurance man thinks he's figured how to beat the market—" Doug and Juliet paid little attention to my moralizing, however.

"So he's hard up, and would probably rather marry a girl with some money, to put it plainly," said Juliet. "Well, that's that. Walter may have been an obstacle in his way—"

"And Walter might have known too much and been keeping still for Madeline's sake," Doug hazarded. "Madeline was struck down pretty near Page's door, and I've always had a sneaking notion that she has an idea who it was. For that matter, she might have put Page up to it."

"He'd certainly do almost anything for her," said Juliet. "And he probably would have been nervous enough to have to shoot twice, but I can't imagine his doing it. But then, I can't imagine anyone doing it."

"One comforting thing, we never lack for theories," said Doug. "Well, I must be getting along. I'll leave you two to exercise your mighty brains in peace."

"I'm tired of thinking," said Juliet almost pettishly and I agreed with her.

Nevertheless we continued to sit in the library, with no other occupation than our thoughts. Juliet was curled up in a large chair, absently drawing meaningless designs on a sheet of paper, while I looked out the window and found myself trying to count the roses on a bush near the house.

I had done this for perhaps the twentieth time when Myra came in with the usual afternoon drink—some sort of fruit punch in this case, which we accepted most gratefully.

"Did you take some to the others?" I said.

Myra had a distressing way of considering me as the nominal head of the household, which must have been irritating to Madeline, so I thought I had as well see that no one was neglected.

"The sheriff ain't back yet. I took some in to Miss Madeline and her beau in the other room—though they're spooning too hard to care about it," said Myra scornfully. "They're gone on each other—if it lasts."

"Don't you think it will?" said Juliet quickly.

"Maybe," said Myra, with her customary caution. "You know what a flirtatious creature Miss Madeline's always been, but I admit that she seems to know her own mind this time. She's just like her mother. Miss Rose was an awful flirt, but when she did see the man she wanted she had to have him right then."

"Does she look like her mother?" I asked. "I never saw Rose King, you know."

"She favors her a lot, only she's considerable more healthy. Miss Rose was always a frail thing. Miss Ellen worried about her a lot. She was always getting bad coughs and wouldn't take care of herself. No wonder she died of consumption."

"She worried about all of them, I imagine," said Juliet, holding out her glass to be refilled. She tried a mild bit of flattery as she had once before. "That's good, Myra. I'd like to know how you make it."

"Miss Ellen showed me, but I haven't got the same knack for mixing things like that as she had."

Something seemed to have caused Myra to relax slightly; perhaps a desire for companionship which might be present even in her dour nature.

"Yes, she did worry about all of them, and no one thanked her for it," she went on. "She was happy enough as a girl, and then everything went wrong at once; her step-mother died, and her father, and Miss Rose up and married—and she went blind."

"And her brother ran away about that time, didn't he?" said Juliet.

"I didn't suppose you knew about him. Yes, he went off, and good riddance," said Myra. "Not but what Miss Ellen felt bad about it. She'd always stood up for him, and then he went into a tantrum because she was to have full charge of the property and he couldn't fling his share away like he wanted."

"What ever became of him?" I asked, with an elaborate pretense of ignorance.

Myra shrugged her shoulders. "There's no knowing. Miss Ellen tried to trace him, and she thought he'd been killed in some riverside saloon—about the kind of place he'd go to, but I always expected him to turn up any time these last twenty years. A bad penny always turns up, but he hasn't so far and I hope he never does."

"If he is alive, why wouldn't he come, home?" said Juliet.

Her usual look of reticence came over Myra's face. "As to that, I couldn't say. There might be reasons. Like as not he is dead," she added. "Do you want any more of this, or shall I take it out with me?"

"Oh, you might as well leave it here. I'll probably sip at it till dinner time," said Juliet. "Dinner may be late if we wait for Doug."

"I'm used to that," said Myra grimly. "But if he ain't here by half past eight, we'll eat without him. I can't wait all night to clean up."

"That's all right," Juliet agreed. Then suddenly: "Myra, is Mr. Trent's cook in the habit of taking a vacation?"

"Not that I know of. Cooks don't generally get vacations," said Myra. "Why, is she gone?"

"He said that he let her go on a vacation yesterday. Is she the only servant he has?"

"The only regular one. He has a man come to do things in the yard and outside the house." Having answered, Myra closed her lips tightly and left the room, as if fearing questions whose significance she could not guess.

"She hates to part with information worse than a Scotchman does with money," Juliet sighed. "Never mind—while we're engaging in trite similes—constant dripping wears away stone."

"I'm afraid that it will take a lot to wear away that stone," I said. "I think I'll see what the others are doing, even at the risk of interrupting what Myra designates as 'spooning.' White should be in presently. He said that he was coming back. Probably Doug will bring him."

But White came and we had had dinner it was ten and then eleven o'clock and still Douglas and Jackson had not returned.

XVII
Douglas's Narrative

I have asked Douglas to tell in his own words what he and Jackson did that night. Juliet says something learned about unity of viewpoint, but I point to *Treasure Island* and she remarks that it probably doesn't matter anyway, as I have already related a number of things which were described to me by others. Therefore, Doug's narrative follows, though he protests that he doesn't know how to write anything but briefs.

I found Jackson waiting for me in front of the village garage which had been a blacksmith shop and had undergone very little change in structure since that time. I thought I had better fill up the gas tank and have the air checked in the tires and while the attendant was doing this Jackson strolled across the street to speak to someone who hailed him.

I could see the elderly fellow who ran the gas tank eying me with open curiosity. It occurred to me that we had left the village and its inhabitants completely out of our calculations. Of course, that was because we had almost at once discounted the idea of an intruder from the outside. Still it was always possible that we were wrong and I began to wonder what, if anything, could be gleaned from the village. So, when the attendant—Jackson called him Bill—said: "Pretty hot today," I responded very cordially that it was. That encouraged him and he ventured:

"They're saying that Walter King wasn't a case of suicide, after all."

There seemed to be no harm in my saying that things pointed the other way, though I guess Jackson wouldn't have been so communicative.

"I can understand folks having a grudge against him, so to speak," said Bill, bending to the tires. "But Miss King, now—that's different. I never knew anyone to say a word against her, 'cepting one man, and he has a spite against the whole family."

"Who's that?" I said, as carelessly as possible. I really wanted to shout it, but he took the question as a matter of course.

"Oh, old Jed Lang. Lives here in town now, but he used to live on the King property up to ten years ago. He took it hard, being put off, but I always understood that he pestered Miss King so much that she had to get rid of him. But Jed ain't just right in his head, lately," Bill added dispassionately. "Not since his daughter died. He takes queer spells."

"What does he do?" I asked.

"Nothing to speak of. He's a locksmith and I guess he picks up a little that way, but not much."

A locksmith. It wouldn't take one to find a key that would fit those antediluvian locks at Hillside, but a locksmith would have easy access to a good many kinds of keys.

"Is he the only one in town?" I said, still with that overdone carelessness that wouldn't have deceived anyone less suspicious than Bill. "I suppose even Miss King had to ask his help sometimes. Keys are always getting lost."

"That's a fact," Bill agreed, washing off the windshield now. "Why, we lost the key to a desk drawer one time, an' where do you suppose we found it? In the craw of a chicken we killed. Yes sir, that's where it was. I guess one of the kids throwed it out in the yard. We all go to Jed when we need anything of that kind; glad to put a little money in his pocket, So I guess Miss King did too."

I could see that Jackson was about to join me so I asked my last question hastily:

"Has his daughter been dead long?"

"'Bout two years, I guess, maybe less. He set great store by her, but she wasn't no good when she was young. Always running around with every Tom, Dick an' Harry, then all the sudden she settled down and didn't appear like she cared if she lived or died, but she lived a long time, at that. Guess she was around forty when she died, but Jed he always seemed to think about her same's if she was still a little girl."

He gave the windshield a final rub with his chamois as Jackson came up and heaved himself into the car.

"Business good, Bill?" he asked.

"Nothin' extra, constable. We get some of the tourists, though, so we got to keep open all night or there's a howl from the customers. Sat'day I stayed here 'cause the boy who usually tends to things wanted off, an' I don't believe there was three cars stopped all night. Mr. Trent, he come by about three o'clock—Sunday morning, that would be."

"Trent did! Three o'clock Sunday morning! In the car! Where was he going?"

Bill looked slightly bewildered at this barrage of questions, but he answered them methodically.

"Sure it was Mr. Trent and naturally he was in a car, and I know it was Sunday mornin'. As to where he was going, I didn't ask him, an' he didn't say, but he wanted some gas in a hurry. His tank was about empty, so I gave him some—"

"Was he alone?"

"Sure, he was alone— Now, wait a minute." Bill stopped and thought, and judging by his face the process was painful. "I didn't see anyone with him, but now I remember he had the curtains down in the back. He's got a see-dan, you know, and it has them inside curtains you can pull down, but folks don't use them much unless they're trying to hide. Mr. Trent did seem in a big hurry and kind of nervous, and it was funny for him to be out that time of night—"

Jackson broke in again.

"Well, at least you know if he went straight ahead toward Anderson or turned off on the Colby road?"

"Oh yes, he went toward Colby. But I started to tell you," said Bill patiently. "I couldn't give him but five gallons, account of being short and having to save for emergencies like, because the gas man was late getting to me and I wasn't sure that he'd turn up that day or Monday—"

"Funny how everything in this world is tied up together," said Jackson. Bill looked at him uncomprehendingly, but he smiled politely at the remark. "So he had five gallons of gas?"

"Not much more than that. His tank was near empty when he come here, and he wanted me to fill it up, but I told him—"

"Yes, yes—thanks," said Jackson hastily. "We'll have to be getting along." But when we started, he said: "Drive slow. I want to think."

We went down the main street, not at all a long distance, and came to where another road branched off from this.

"Shall I take the road to Colby?" I said innocently.

Jackson looked at me and grinned.

"Well, what about it? It may be a wild goose chase, but I'd like to know why Trent was chasing around the country at three o'clock Sunday morning. It's no crime to take a ride at that time, of course, but it certainly isn't his regular habit. Go on, turn—no, wait a minute. Go straight ahead to that big white house down there. It's the hospital and I think I'll go in while we're here."

When we stopped to my surprise he invited me to come in with him and we ascended the broad steps and went into a small, square office just off the entrance hall. The nurse in charge there objected to our going up, but after some insistence on Jackson's part she yielded and we went on to one of the private rooms, where Miss Barnes met us at the door. She also looked at us disapprovingly, and shook her head at Jackson's question.

"Just the same, though he's resting fairly well, and at least I know that he is safe here," she said. "Yes, he talks some, but very little more than I reported to Mr. White, and nothing that makes sense." In fact, we could hear the low, toneless murmur of Mark's voice from where we stood, but not clearly enough to distinguish words.

"I'd like to go inside," said Jackson, after vainly straining his ears to hear. "Oh, no, I couldn't have him disturbed," said Miss Barnes firmly. "He must not be bothered in any way and he must have absolute quiet."

"We won't disturb or speak to him," said Jackson, with equal determination. "We'll only go near enough to hear what he's saying, but I do want to hear that."

Miss Barnes looked as if she meditated closing the door in his face, but he brushed by her while she was still undecided and I followed closely. We stopped just inside the door, as the room was small and pretty well filled by the narrow bed, a table and chair. Mark's face—that part of it which was not hidden by the crisscross of white bandages—was turned toward us, pallid and sunken looking, his eyes closed. His lips moved steadily in a meaningless mutter of words:

"Burning, burning—Ellen, Walter—what are you burning—don't! don't!—burning, burning—tell them—where's Ellen—don't! don't!—burning—what are you burning—"

I think we must have listened to this for over five minutes, with very little variation, while Miss Barnes stood with a glacial eye fixed on us. Then Jackson sighed, evidently resisting a strong impulse to try to direct Mark's ravings to some purpose, and stepped back into the hall. His polite, "Thank you, nurse," brought only a short nod from Miss Barnes, and we went out to the car again.

"Now, go back and turn toward Colby," Jackson said, when we were on our way again: "Well, we got very little help there. Lord, if that boy could only talk! But did you notice one thing? He said: 'Ellen, Walter, what are you burning?' Sometimes I'm inclined to believe that the two murders may not be connected at all, but that Walter King was guilty."

"But you didn't quote Mark's words correctly," I said. "He did say just what you repeated, but not the same way. He said 'Ellen, Walter—' Then he paused before he said 'What are you burning?' It makes a lot of difference."

"I suppose so," Jackson agreed gloomily. "I guess you're right, though it would be simpler if I could convince myself he did say 'Walter, what are you burning?' But as to King's murder, have you considered that Miss West is going to inherit half his share now?"

"You mean she might have done it for that reason?"

"Well, it's a possibility. She could have done it without having anything to do with Miss King's death," said Jackson. "But I wasn't thinking just of her— I doubt if she did it, myself. I think she was pretty fond of him, and there's Page, you know. But he's pretty well off himself, so—"

I debated within myself, then:

"No, he's not pretty well off," I said. "He got cleaned in the stock market, according to recent information, and has only his salary, which is on a commission basis, and things are pretty tight just now."

"So-o!" Jackson whistled. "I wish you amateur detectives would pass along all these little tips you get," he remarked. "We aren't holding out on you, so you might make it a fifty-fifty proposition, don't you think?"

I found myself turning red.

"Amateur detectives?" I echoed feebly.

"Sure—you and Miss Selby and Mr. Haynes. Think I didn't know you three have been trying to puzzle things out? That's all right with me, but if you've learned anything vital you might pass it along."

"Well—" I decided not to tell about Ellen's diary for the simple reason that I feared the eminently practical Jackson would ridicule us. "There's a conversation Mr. Haynes overheard between Walter and Page, in which Page warned Walter to keep away from Madeline. He said it would be the last warning he gave him, which may very well have been only a manner of speaking."

"That old guy certainly hears things," Jackson muttered. "'Scuse me, he's a friend of yours and I like him fine myself. Go on."

"Well, that's all, except the talk I had with your friend Bill back there, and I was going to tell you about that as soon as I had a chance. He was telling me that some old customer named Jed Long has a grudge against the King family, and that he's a locksmith."

"Jed Long? I know him. He isn't quite—normal," said Jackson thoughtfully. "And since you speak of it, I remember hearing he did have no good words for the Kings. But how could he get in, any more than anyone else? A locksmith, you say? Um-m."

"Of course we found no footprints about the house, in spite of the damp ground."

"No, not where we looked carefully, which was under Miss King's windows, on the supposition that someone might have climbed up by way of those vines," said Jackson. "If anyone used the regular paths to the doors, those are very well graveled. We've never considered anyone from the outside gaining entrance with a key, but it would be fairly simple, if this thing was planned far enough ahead to allow of one being procured somehow. That confounded system of locking up the house! It's as bad for us as those upper porches have been. Let's see, the door was locked that night?"

"Myra says so. But the other time we found the key out of the lock."

"It's easy enough to do. The key could be replaced and then a window opened—" Jackson smiled in a shamefaced fashion. "There's where I slipped up. We examined the windows in the front rooms, but I didn't get a look at those in the dining room or kitchen before the servants had already raised them for the day. Of course, there's always the possibility that someone inside the house let a person in from outside. I'd like to know if Myra knows this Long, and I'll find out when I get around to him. Now, as to Trent—if you had five gallons of gas in the tank, what would you be most likely to do?"

"Stop at the first gas station and get some more," I said promptly. "Ask me another."

"What would you estimate to the gallon?"

"Oh, Lord knows. You can't judge by this bus of mine. It eats gas. Trent has a Buick sedan. About twelve miles to a gallon would be a good average, I'd say."

"Sixty miles he could go, then," said Jackson. "But I'm counting on his having stopped before that. Besides, he can't have made such a very long trip, because I was over there Sunday morning about nine o'clock talking to his cook, and he was there then. She didn't know he had been gone, either, or she would have told me. If he's up to something he didn't want known, it's no wonder he was willing for her to take a vacation."

We came to the first of the many intersecting roads along the way.

"Where do we go now?" I said, as I stopped, seeing that there were at least five towns within a radius of fifty miles.

Jackson frowned, and it certainly wasn't an easy decision to make.

"I'm blamed if I know," he said helplessly. "He might have turned off, or gone straight ahead to any of these places. How do we know? Well, three of them aren't as large as Hillside, and let's say for the sake of argument that he'd have no reason for making a trip to a one-horse town that would be asleep from nine o'clock on. He might have turned off here toward Millton, or gone on to Colby. But I remember there's a gas station several miles straight ahead so we might as well keep on."

However, when we reached the service station, we drew a blank, for the owner said that he closed down at ten and didn't open before six in the morning. After some indecision, Jackson told me to go ahead on the same road.

It was only thirty miles to Colby and Trent could have made it on what gas he had. It took us a little over half an hour to get there—I was in no danger of speed cops since I had a constable with me, I thought—and I was giving her all she could take.

Colby was not precisely a metropolis, but it was a thriving town compared with Hillside and had a large enough number of garages and gas stations that it took some time for Jackson to cover them all. The nearest approach to success that he had was with a freckled kid at an all-night station, who remembered a mysterious closed car that he was sure must be in the bootlegging traffic. He was painfully anxious to please Jackson with his description of the driver, and would have followed any leads given him very eagerly, but when Jackson made him stick to what he actually could remember—or thought he could—his picture of the driver certainly did not resemble Trent.

However, we thanked him and I bought some more gas and tipped him fairly well, and we decided to get something to eat, as it was after seven and apparently our search had just begun. We found a fairly decent looking quick lunch place and over his steak and French fries, Jackson growled disgustedly:

"Here we are, forty miles from home and none the wiser. If I'd had any sense I would have told you to drive to Trent's and asked him out and out where he was. That will probably be what I'll have to do in the end, as it is."

XVIII

Douglas's Narrative Continued

The steak and potatoes, with a large slab of apple pie and three cups of coffee, fortified Jackson somewhat for the task ahead of him, and when we had finished eating he tackled it with new energy.

"Trent wouldn't dare to go any further than here on what gas he had," he reasoned. "Of course there's always a chance he did fill up here and no one remembers. In that case, we lose him, but he couldn't have gone very far and returned when he did. So we'd better argue that he didn't come here and go back and try the Millton road."

"Aren't there roads turning off on it?" I asked.

"Yes, there's one to Kelsey," Jackson admitted. "But that's about forty miles away. We'll see if there's any small places fairly near the turn off where he might have stopped for gas and we'll try Millton. If that fails, we'd better call it a day. He could get to Millton on five gallons, but he couldn't get back."

I had had a very solid piece of apricot pie which already felt like a stone dropped in my middle, and I was not so optimistic as Jackson now.

"Just as you say, but suppose he has been there? What then?"

"I'll find out why," said Jackson. "There must be a reason for a jaunt like that at three o'clock in the morning."

Since Jackson was determined I gave up grumbling as a bad job and we went back to the Millton road at much the same pace we had come. About five miles out on the highway we came to the Kelsey road, but the nearest town named on the signboard was twenty miles distant and Jackson could not remember any stations along the way, so he gave the word to go on.

Everything went nicely until we got a stretch marked "detour—road under construction."

I cussed, shifted gears and took the detour, which must have been used for cow pastures most of its life. I gave Jackson a good bumping and I'm not sure he didn't hit the top once, but I figured that it was his picnic as much as mine.

We finally slid in and out of an unusually deep gully so deep that I was afraid we had done some damage to the car, which is lower slung than the average. So when we lurched out of the detour and onto the highway again, I stopped to investigate.

By causing me to do so, that detour was the first luck to come our way. A young fellow in a Ford coupe had seen us coming and waited until we got out of it to tackle the road himself. When he saw me get out of the car to take a look at things, he came over, too, and asked if he could help.

"No, there doesn't seem to be anything wrong," I said. "I was afraid we might have scraped the pan in that last ditch."

"It's a tough stretch of road, all right, but you get used to it," he said. "It's worse coming over it in the dark, too. Fellow broke a spring driving by here last Saturday—Sunday morning, it really was."

You could see Jackson pricking up his ears.

"What time Sunday?" he said. "Very late—or early?"

The youngster grinned.

"Early is the best word. It was along about four o'clock, because I was coming back from a dance in Millton and I didn't leave till after three. He hit this same chuck hole here, and he thought the car was on the bum for good, but I got out my flashlight and helped him take a look, and just one of the middle leaves of the spring was broken, so he was able to go on. I guess he was driving pretty fast, because he seemed to be in a hurry to get along."

"Anybody with him?" said Jackson. "What did he look like?"

The young chap looked surprised, but he answered good naturedly.

"I didn't see anybody with him, but I remember the curtains were down in the back of the car and on one side in front. Didn't think much about it at the time. Friend of yours? Oh-h!"

Jackson had showed his badge.

"Why, it was dark, of course, so I didn't see him so awfully well, but he was a nice looking fellow with a little mustache. Some gray in it, I think. I couldn't see his hair on account of his hat."

"That's near enough to satisfy us," said Jackson. "Are there any towns of any size between here and Millton?"

"Not on this road, and if you turn of at the cross roads down there it's nearly thirty-five miles to Deming. By the way, he asked about service stations, and I told him there was one at the cross roads, but he'd have to wake old Pete up to get gas. He said he didn't know if he had enough to get into Millton or not."

"Thanks, we'll stop there," said Jackson. I guess the kid wondered to the end of his days what it was all about, but he probably thought we were chasing bootleggers.

The crossroads were only a few miles from there and here we found one of these service stations where you can get gas, oil, cigarettes, spare Ford parts, ham sandwiches and soda water.

"I guess I do remember this fellow you speak of," said the grimy attendant, as he cranked more gas into my car, which I let Jackson pay for, incidentally. "He woke me up about four o'clock, or after four, I guess it was. Anyhow, I was plenty sore about it, but long's I was awake, I figured I might as well make a dollar or so. Yes, it was a sedan, and I remember some of the curtains were pulled down. I suppose it's one of them guys who peddle booze that you're after? I thought something about that at the time, but if a fellow wants gas I give it to him."

"Sure, why not?" said Jackson amiably. "Good thing, sometimes—helps us to trail them. Now what," he added, as we went on, "do you suppose our friend Trent was doing over here? Since we seem likely to trace him, I'm beginning to wonder what it's all about."

"Maybe he *is* bootlegging," I suggested facetiously.

"Trent?" Jackson snorted. "He has the name around the village of being a strict teetotaler."

"Most bootleggers—wise ones, at least—are."

Jackson snorted again.

"I guess you don't mean me to take you seriously, but this is no time for joking, Martin, and I wonder what he went to Millton for."

"Can't you find out when we get there?—if he didn't turn off some other place, after all."

"Maybe." Jackson did not sound too hopeful. "One good thing, he probably had to stop at a garage about that spring. But he must have come back pretty quick, to get home in time."

We had been over this ground so often before that I didn't bother to answer, and we got to Millton in another half hour. We drew blank at the first four garages and two stations before we stopped before one which had a prominent "open all night" sign.

To Jackson's question, a mechanic said that he wasn't on the night shift, but Dave Braden was, and he'd be in about nine-thirty. But Jackson wouldn't wait, so we were directed to Braden's house and found him watering the lawn.

"Yes, he'd been on night shift last Saturday and Sunday," he said. "Fellow with a broken spring? Sure, he stopped in the garage about five o'clock Sunday morning. The spring wasn't broken bad, so I sort of clamped it so's it wouldn't spread, and he went on. He said he had to drive in a hurry to get home, so he wouldn't wait to have it fixed here. What did he look like? Well, he was medium built, and kind of middle aged, with a gray mustache—"

"That's him," said Jackson. "Was there anyone with him?"

"No, he was all alone."

"You're sure of that? Weren't the side curtains down in the car?"

"No, they wasn't," said Dave, "I'd a noticed if they had been, because I got a jack out of the back of the car."

"All right. Thanks," said Jackson, and we drove off, leaving our friend Dave to stare after us as most of our previous informants had.

After we had gone several blocks, Jackson motioned me to draw up to the curb and sat there in unhappy silence.

"Now we are up against a blind wall. We can't ask everyone in town if they saw him. Darned few of them would've been awake and on the streets, anyway. I might have known he'd stop on his way out of town, instead of when he came in."

"We might go back and ask Trent—perhaps it would save time in the end," I said.

I admit I was tiring of the chase, and besides, I had a hunch that we might be following a side issue and neglecting the more vital one. Not Jackson, however.

"No," he said, setting his jaw. "Let me think a bit first. Then if I have to go back and ask Trent with the risk of getting everything but the truth—all right."

While he thought, I looked for a cigarette, discovered that it was my last one and went across the street to a drug store to buy more. When I came back Jackson was still slumped down in the car, frowning ferociously.

"I've been thinking," he announced unnecessarily. "Let's take this thing a step at a time. Saturday night was the time someone tried to scare the bunch of you with that tapping stunt down the hall. What time did that happen?"

"Oh, it was between twelve and one o'clock, I think."

"Yes, and then Trent leaves town about three and comes over here. Some connection—maybe. White thinks someone was outside the house that night; we find the key on the floor—someone might have entered the house.

If it was Trent, after something, why did he have to come over here afterward?"

"I don't know, but it doesn't make any sense," I said.

"I know it doesn't," Jackson agreed. "Well, next morning we find Trent's footprints in the garden, probably made the night before."

"And you found the prints of someone you haven't identified."

"That's so." Jackson started suddenly. "Say—that's so! Wait a minute—let me think."

I felt inclined to tell him that I wasn't hindering him, but kept it to myself. So far as my own brain power was concerned, it seemed to be nil.

"Drive to the railroad station," said Jackson finally, "It's on down the street toward the end of town."

I obeyed, without the least idea what he was after now, and when we reached there it was to inquire about trains leaving the town between four-thirty and sir o'clock in the morning. There was only one, the station agent said, and it was an express which had to be flagged if it stopped there. No, it hadn't stopped Sunday.

"Well," said Jackson, "how about the next train? When is that? Ten o'clock? Do you remember any stranger leaving town on it Sunday morning?"

The agent looked at him scornfully.

"That's the popular train, that and the three o'clock. There might have been half a dozen strangers leave and wouldn't have time to notice them."

"I see," said Jackson, heavily. "Well—thanks."

"What's the idea?" I said, as we got into the car again. "Who's the mysterious stranger?"

"Damned if I know. It was just a hunch gone wrong. Those other prints—see! Suppose it was someone Trent wanted to get away, so he wouldn't risk letting him go from Hillside, but brought him over here to catch a train—"

"Oh, I see." I took my foot off the starter, struck by a sudden idea, and made my one and only contribution the evening's work. "Suppose, on the other hand, that he and Trent collided and Trent wanted to get him out of the way? Is there a hospital here?"

Jackson's face lighted slowly.

"That's another hunch, a pretty wild one, but worth trying. Sure there's a hospital. Turn to your right at the next street. I think I remember where it is. I chased over here after some auto thieves once."

We found the hospital, a fine brown, stucco building, easily enough and located the office. Jackson showed his badge immediately, probably anticipating trouble.

"We're looking for a man who was brought here early Sunday morning by another man who probably didn't give his real name."

The office nurse consulted her records.

"Yes, there was a man brought in about four-thirty Sunday. He was booked under the name of Mr. Knight.

His companion—he said his name was Gray—told us that
he and Knight had been on a motoring trip because of a
nervous breakdown Knight had suffered, and that he had
had a bad relapse, so he thought he had better leave him
here. There were some queer features about the case, but
Mr. Gray paid us in advance and promised to come back
soon, so we admitted his friend."

"Were you here? Can you describe Gray, as you call him?"

"I wasn't on duty, but I'll call the nurse who was here
that night. Is there any difficulty, officer? Is the man wanted for something?"

"I couldn't tell you that right now," Jackson evaded. "Is
he badly injured?"

"Injured? Oh no, not at all," said the nurse. "He seems
to be suffering from shock and exhaustion, and is in a
very run-down condition. In fact, we would imagine that
he had led a life of dissipation for some time. He was very
poorly dressed, they tell me, which seemed queer, because
Mr. Gray was obviously a gentleman, and yet he said they
were out on a trip together. We thought perhaps Knight
was a man of some standing, who had gotten into some
trouble and his friend was helping him out and keeping it
hidden."

"That's a pretty good guess," said Jackson. "When the
nurse comes, could we take a look at this fellow, to identify him?"

"I'll see if it is possible. Oh, Miss Billings. You were
on duty here Sunday and this gentleman—Mr. Jackson—
would like to have you describe Mr. Gray."

"Oh, he was very nice," said Miss Billings, wide-eyed.
"He was a middle-aged man, dressed very nicely, with iron
gray hair and a close-cropped mustache."

Jackson nodded, as I murmured: "Blessings on the mustache."

"Are you in charge of Knight's case, by any chance?" he said. "You are? Well, could we take a look at him?"

"I'm sure it wouldn't hurt anything, if you are quiet and don't talk to him," said Miss Billings. "He is not to be disturbed, you see, but I think he is asleep just now. Shall I take them up, Miss Sears?"

Miss Sears said she should, and we followed the nurse up the stairs and through the hallway to a small ward.

"Shock and exhaustion, you say?" Jackson asked as we went.

"Yes. The doctor says that he has been drinking heavily for some time, and there is a certain mental instability that is apt to lead to a thing like this breakdown. He hasn't seemed to have any curiosity about where he is or what is going on. and he's slept a good deal of the time."

"Does he talk?"

"He doesn't actually talk, but sometimes he becomes restless in his sleep and murmurs one name a good deal."

"What is the name?" said Jackson, with barely suppressed eagerness.

"Ellen. He is the one in the second bed. Please don't go too close."

The man in the bed was no one we knew; of medium height and very thin, with a dark face faintly lined, and dark hair a little long from lack of barbering. He slept motionlessly, but now and then his forehead wrinkled as if something puzzled him. Jackson took a good look, thanked Miss Billings and we left.

"Ever see him before?" he said in the hall.

"Never."

"Remind you of anyone?"

"Who, for instance?" I temporized.

"Walter King," said Jackson. "It hit me in the face as soon as I looked at him. Well?"

I myself was so struck by that resemblance and by what it might mean that I did not answer immediately. So many things went through my mind at the sight of that strange, yet familiar face, that it seemed to me that minutes must have passed while, with Jackson's heavy bewildered gaze upon me, I pondered the significance of this return of the prodigal.

For this was beyond any possibility of doubt, Philip King. There was a chance that I, who knew of his existence and had been thinking no little about him only a short time before, might jump to a hasty conclusion because of a merely superficial likeness. After all, the light in the ward had been quite dim, and men may have eyes and noses and mouths of the same cast without being brothers.

But Jackson's statement to me convinced me that my first wild surmise had been right. Jackson had no knowledge of the existence of a missing brother, as far as I knew, and he lacked also the swift imagination that would link the sad wreck on the bed with the headstrong and proud boy who had gone away so long. No, if Jackson saw immediately that he looked like Walter, it must be more than mere resemblance that made him see it. It must be something as strong as a blood tie. I spoke at last, almost to myself.

"Juliet said she'd wager Walter looked like him," I muttered. "She also said she didn't like him cropping up; the long-lost brother who always appears so miraculously. And here he is."

"Here who is! What are you talking about?" said Jackson, "Are you still holding out on me?"

"Not at all. I supposed you knew that Miss King had a younger brother, Philip, who ran away when he was a youngster," I said mendaciously.

"Well, I didn't," said Jackson. "Go on."

"She couldn't trace him, and so far as anyone knows, didn't hear from him all this time."

"Why did he leave?"

"The only reason we know is because he was angry when Ellen's father gave her charge of the estate. But he was wild and extravagant, anyway."

"And you think this fellow here is Philip King?"

"Well, you said yourself how much he looks like Walter King."

"Maybe it's accidental, his turning up—maybe not," Jackson muttered. "Anyway, we'll find out. There's a lot I've got to ask Trent."

Then—to strain coincidence to the breaking point—we came to the front door and face to face with Edward Trent.

XIX

Ellen's Brother

If Trent was greatly surprised or discomfited, he did not
show it in any way, but greeted us with a cool "good evening," and waited for Jackson to make the first move,
which he did, by remarking casually:

"We've just been up to see your friend."

"Indeed! How is he?" said Trent.

"He's sleeping right now, and they say he's getting
along all right, so maybe you won't want to waste your
time going up."

Trent looked at him with an ironical smile.

"I can come back when you are through with me," he
said. "I suppose you do want to talk to me?"

"Well, it can wait until we get home, if you like," said
Jackson politely. "But naturally I've got a few questions
to ask."

"I understand that and I had as well answer them here.
Suppose we go to restaurant. I know of one where we can
have a private booth."

"That will be all right. I could stand a sandwich and
cup of coffee," said Jackson, ignoring my subdued groan.

The cafe was one of those consisting of a long lunch
counter and "booths for ladies." We took a booth toward
the rear, attended by an interested waiter, and talked as-
siduously about the weather until our orders had arrived.

Trent made small pretense of touching his food and the pie was still too much with me to allow of my enjoying it, but Jackson interspersed his questions with mouthfuls of sandwich and more coffee.

Trent, however, began the conversation.

"You know who the man I brought to the hospital is?"

"Well, we took a guess. That is, I said he looked like Walter King and Martin here guessed he might be Miss King's brother."

"I didn't suppose you knew that Miss King had a brother," said Trent. "She never spoke of him, except to me."

"Well, Mr. Haynes has known the family a long time," I said quickly; too quickly, for Trent gave me a glance that said "I'd like to know how much you know"—or so I figured it.

"Mr. Haynes didn't know him," he said. "But Miss King may very well have spoken of him. Yes, that is Philip King in the hospital—home after wandering God knows where."

"Why did he stay away so long, and come back just now?" said Jackson.

Trent frowned, but did not answer his implication immediately.

"You know why he went away in the first place?"

"Well, Martin gave me an idea, but I'd like to hear it from you."

"Oh, so you—I mean, Haynes—had heard that, too?" said Trent. "He went very soon after his father died, because Miss King was given charge of the estate, instead of Philip and Rose being independent. No one could blame old Mr. King for that; Phil and Rose had both always been irresponsible and extravagant, while Ellen was the level headed one. Well, Philip raged about it, quarreled with Ellen and went out of the house with threats, which was entirely characteristic of him, I may say. Miss King supposed he would soon come back, rather the worse for several days of liquor and gambling—"

"And he didn't," Jackson finished.

"No, he didn't. There was no word from him and no trace of him, but they thought some unidentified body found in the river at that time might be his, and Miss King really gave him up as dead. She didn't ever think of any reason for his going but anger about the will," said Trent. "But I'm going to be frank with you and say that I've sometimes wondered if he might not have had other reasons that prompted him to stay away for a time, after he had gone away in a fit of anger over his father's will."

"Reasons—such as?" Jackson said.

Trent reddened a little.

"Philip was never popular in the village. In those days the King family had more or less the same relation to the town as an old feudal family to a village, and Philip was apt to avail himself of the young lord's privilege with the village girls. I don't know of any definite charge ever being brought against him, but he was mixed up with two or three—"

"Names?" said Jackson quickly.

Trent hesitated.

"I only recall one—Jed Lang's daughter. Of course, her reputation was never very wholesome, so one can't pin too much faith to rumors."

"Naturally not," said Jackson, with what I considered amazing stolidity. "Still, you can't help wondering what kept him away so many years when there was money and comfort at home."

"Oh, I don't think that is so difficult," said Trent rather impatiently. "Not if you know Philip King as I did. He probably had a healthy resentment against his sister to begin with and dreams of 'showing her' by winning a fortune of his own. When he didn't, he was ashamed to come home, and he is the type who finds drifting easier than direct action. The way I see it, he probably went on drifting; half ashamed to come home. Besides, there was a wandering streak in the family before now, that cropped up sometimes."

"That's all right, as far as it goes, but I'll be frank with you, too, Mr. Trent, and say it seems queer that he should happen home just at this particular time."

"I know," said Trent. "And though stranger things have happened, I will admit I felt that, too—at least, I felt that you might see it in that light, and that is why I got him out of the way, until I could think things over, and to give him a chance to recover a bit."

"Yes, and that brings us to the question—what is wrong with him, Trent?"

"I'll have to tell you all I know, and it is rather a long story, but I'll try to be as concise as possible," said Trent. "It was Saturday morning, as you know, that all of us were at Hillside for your questioning. In the afternoon I sat around the house and—well, I sat there all afternoon and after dinner until about ten o'clock. Mamie—the cook— was in bed, and I finally decided I must at least try to sleep and went to latch the front door, when a man stepped up on the porch. I knew at once that it was Philip King, though he was very poorly dressed, and much older, of course, besides being changed in other ways.

"He said 'Hello, Ed,' as if it had been the day before and not twenty years since we had spoken. I was too surprised to do anything but hold open the door for him to come in. Then he said: 'Well, I thought I'd come around to you first, to break the shock.'

"It didn't take me more than that long to see that he wasn't completely sober.

"So when he said 'How is Ellen?' I was in a quandary. It wasn't alone his being a little—drunk, but he impressed me as being in a condition of nervous irritability, and I was afraid of the effect of my—news upon him. And besides, I must admit, I shrank from the thought of the scene there would be when I told him of Ellen's death. I felt I had had all I could bear for one day and that it would be better to tell him in the morning what had happened."

"Sure, that was natural enough," Jackson agreed. "Then what?"

"Well, it's queer how one runs to inanities in an unusual situation. I asked him when he got in—"

"Yes?" said Jackson quickly. "And when did he?"

"He didn't give me a straight answer," said Trent reluctantly. "But I got the impression he had been around Hillside for a day, but was too intoxicated to appear. I tried to get something of the story of the last twenty years from him, but his answers were pretty vague, and about all I gathered was that he had been over the seven seas on every kind of vessel. Finally I asked him why he came home now. He said he was getting too old to 'rough it' and he had come home to—" Trent hesitated, then: "'to get what was coming to him'," he finished. "Those were the words he used and naturally I said that he could have had it any time within the last twenty years, and he said: 'Sure, but I think I'm old enough now that there shouldn't be any apron strings about the business. I'll bet Rose has had hers like she wanted it right along'.

"Then I had to tell him that Rose was dead. Naturally that was difficult, and as soon as he had recovered he wanted to go straight to Ellen. He said: 'I thought it would be a good joke to let myself in and surprise her in the morning'."

"Let himself in?" Jackson sat up straight, almost overturning his coffee cup. "How?"

Trent's reluctance to answer was never more manifest. "It seems he still had his door key. Some strange freak made him carry it about all these years. I think he'd always had the idea of coming home and 'surprising' everyone. People are like that, you know. Anyway, I had a hard time persuading him he'd better stay with me and go over in the morning. As often as I thought I had put him off, he would swing back to the idea of letting himself in and surprising Ellen. I told him there were people staying there, and finally I remembered another thing he didn't know and said, 'Besides, I must prepare Ellen for your being here. She couldn't see you if you did go in—she is blind.'"

Trent sighed and straightened his shoulders, which had unconsciously sagged a little.

"Then—naturally I had to quiet him again, after that, and that seemed to settle it; though it was hard to reason with him because of his condition. I persuaded him to go to bed, and went myself. Naturally, I didn't feel a great deal like sleep, and for some reason I began to feel, after a while, that everything wasn't all right. So I went down to his room and found that he was gone. He had left an empty flask there," Trent added grimly, "so I judged he had been drinking more, which wasn't hopeful. But I hadn't much doubt where to follow him, so I got into my clothes again and started for Hillside.

"The house was perfectly quiet when I reached there, and I crept around it as quietly as I could, hoping Philip had not gone in yet. I was sure the front door must be locked, and if the key was left in it he would have to knock it out to use his. Before I was around to the front of the house again, I could hear a faint disturbance inside—but only faintly, and then Philip came running away from the house. I caught him and held him there for a few minutes, until I saw lights flash on. I didn't know what was happening, then, and didn't dare try to find out, so I pulled Philip away toward home.

"He seemed greatly sobered by what had happened and he kept asking, 'What's wrong! What's going on in there!' I think my nerves snapped, because I told him, brutally, that I didn't know, that Ellen had been killed the night before and that he must keep away from there.

"Well, as I had feared, in his state he nearly collapsed and I had all I could do to get him back. I had to answer some of his questions and that only made him worse. So I made a desperate resolution, and a foolish one, I think now. A hospital was plainly the place for him, and I didn't want to take him there, so I bundled him into the car—he was easy to handle by then—and brought him here. And that's the story."

"All right, as far as it goes," said Jackson. "But I've some questions to ask."

Trent's fingers tightened on his unused table knife, but he nodded.

"I supposed you would have. Go ahead."

"You're pretty sure King got in the night before?"

"I didn't say the night before," Trent corrected quickly. "I think he was around Hillside before he came to me. He didn't say how long."

"We can ask him, of course. He was excited, you said?"

"Well—not precisely normal. I think he had been drinking heavily, and probably for some time."

"And he seemed determined to have his full share of his father's property now?"

"Yes—yes, I think that he was determined on that," said Trent slowly.

"Well, I put it to you, Mr. Trent—if he had demanded that and Miss King refused—"

"But his coming in would have made a great deal of disturbance that late at night," Trent protested. "Miss King couldn't have seen and recognized him at once. There would have had to be explanations and a great deal of talking."

"Then let's put it another way. Suppose that he had cherished this grievance for some years, and being as much under the influence of liquor as he was, found his way home and to her room?"

Trent was silent, then:

"That is the only way it could have been," he said. "He did have a grievance, but if he had talked to her first— But in that case, you must account for the gun."

"Yes, but we are not entirely certain that Walter King's gun was used. It certainly seemed likely, but it may not have been his that we found, though in that case we don't know where his disappeared to."

"You're quite right, but still I can't think that Philip was in any way connected with this affair," said Trent, "I think that it is merely an unhappy coincidence that he came back at this particular time. If he had done it, he would have been lacking in all sense not to have left town at once, instead of coming to me, though I suppose you might attribute that to liquor."

"Exactly. He might not even remember what he had done," said Jackson.

"But if he could gain entrance with his key, how could he get out again and leave the key in the door?"

"We agreed that—due to my carelessness—anyone might have done that by going through a window. Unfortunately they were not all inspected that first morning, because we didn't think of anyone entering with a key. Besides was the key in the door? I don't remember. Myra said she locked up, but we didn't ask her about the other. However, Mr. Trent, don't let this worry you too much. I'll be over in the morning to see if I can talk to King, but I don't feel that he is necessarily involved. The case against him now is pretty weak, and we have other lines to follow. By the way, one more question—what were you burning Saturday afternoon?"

Trent stiffened, then relaxed with an effort.

"I was burning letters that had passed between Miss King and myself at various times," he said, flushing angrily. "Purely personal matters that I would not care to have fall into anyone's hands after I was gone."

"All right, sorry to be so curious," said Jackson. "What time is it? After nine? Well, I think we'd better all be getting home."

"You mean you would rather I wouldn't see King until you have? Very well. Let me congratulate you on tracing me here," said Trent pleasantly. "It must have been something of a task."

"It was hard enough, but not so hard as trying to figure out *why* you came," said Jackson. "Martin here thought you might have gone in for bootlegging, but I absolved you of that, knowing that you never go in for the stuff."

"No—no, I don't," said Trent. "By the way, when you are considering Philip King, don't forget that it would be impossible for him to have anything to do with Walter King's death."

"I don't. But sometimes I think his death isn't connected with Miss King's, and we'll have to conduct an entirely separate inquiry on that. Well—good night."

"Good night," said Trent, with unfailing politeness. "If you'll wait, you can be sure I've gone ahead of you."

"He gets in some sharp digs in that polite way of his," Jackson remarked, climbing into the car. "No, we won't wait. Let her go."

I "let her go," all right, to such an extent that Jackson protested he would just as leave return alive instead of in an ambulance.

"I suppose you're anxious to get home," he said forgivingly. "We've had a hard evening of it, and I'm blessed if I know yet just where it's got us."

"Nowhere," I said grumpily. "I think we've wasted a fine large amount of time, and a good many gallons of gas. 'Long Lost Brother Returns Home' makes a swell headline, but I believe, that's about all it will come to."

"Maybe. We'll see," said Jackson cautiously.

We made the rest of the trip in silence, as I devoted myself to driving and Jackson to thought—or perhaps he was only asleep. It was a little after ten and I was just engaged in comfortable anticipations of bed, when Jackson spoke again and shattered my dream.

"Are you very tired, Martin?"

"Oh—middling," I said unsuspiciously.

"Well, I was just thinking—I want to go over to Millton early tomorrow morning, but I'm also anxious not to put off seeing Jed Long any more than possible. So I thought you might drive me over to his place tonight," he finished blandly.

I groaned. "Good Lord! Can't you send White over there tomorrow morning?"

"White is my boss—theoretically. He can send me wherever he wants, but he's an easy man to work for. He's a fine fellow," said Jackson. "But he's too soft-hearted, White is. He's lived here too long and knows everyone as a friend, so it's hard for him to keep at folks and pester them with questions. It doesn't bother me. I've gone after the bootleggers in this town too hard to be popular with a number of people. So if you'll drive me over to Long's, I think I'll just talk to him now."

"All right, I'll take you there," I said. "But don't expect me to go over to Millton in the morning. You'll have to hire a taxi for that."

"Oh, my own bus will be working then," said Jackson. "Turn at Elm street and go down to the end of it. This is

the nearest thing to an alley or slums that Hillside village
boasts. I think he has a sign in front of his house."

This block differed slightly from the other wide shady
village streets, in that the houses were closer together,
smaller and newer and not lawn-surrounded like the older
houses. In front of one rather untidy gray structure a
clumsy representation of a key swung on an equally home-
made sign.

"Suppose he isn't up?" I said.

"He is, though—in the back end of the house. We'll go
around there; he's probably too deaf to hear us knock. I've
always had vague suspicions," said Jackson, as we picked
our way through the neglected side yard, "that Long makes
a little private stock, and probably sells some of it, too."

He knocked several times before a tall old man, with
a seamed, dark face and gray hair almost to his powerful
stooped shoulders, opened the door and looked at us sus-
piciously from under his bushy eyebrows.

"You know me—Jackson? All right, we'll come in, as
I've got a few questions to ask you."

The room into which we stepped seemed to be a combined kitchen and work room. The windows were closed;
it was stifling hot, and the place was strewn with tools
connected with a key-smith's work. I took off my hat and
fanned myself and Jackson's already limp collar gave up
entirely in the atmosphere. Old Long did not invite us to
be seated, but we sat, anyway.

"I want to know if you can give an account of your time
for the night Miss King was murdered—last Friday night,"
said Jackson, opening the battle without any preliminary
skirmishing.

"I want to know what th' hell business it is of yours?"
said the old man fiercely. "Why should I be connected up
with that killin'?"

"I believe it is true that you had a grudge against the entire King family?" said Jackson. "You have often expressed yourself as hating 'the whole pack of them.'"

"An' I do," said Long calmly. "I've no use or kindness for them or theirs and ain't had for twenty years, and ain't afraid to say so. But I'm not one who'd shoot a blind woman, for all that."

"That sounds well, but you haven't accounted for your time Friday night," said Jackson, unmoved. The old fellow's eyes blazed.

"No," he said witheringly. "No more could any ten men you asked to, if they'd spent an evening at home and went to bed as usual. There's folks saw me down town early, but too early for the time you're interested in."

"How long have you lived here?" said Jackson, letting Long's answer stand, somewhat to my surprise.

"About ten years, come Winter," said the old man.

"Why did Miss King make you leave the estate?"

"We couldn't get along. She said I bothered her with lies. She wasn't all to blame," said Long, with some dignity. "She was loyal to her kin, and I was loyal to mine."

For the minute Jackson let that pass, too.

"Then for ten years you've worked as a locksmith? Did Miss King give you any work?"

"She sent Myra once or twice with extra keys—to have more cut," said Long. "Mostly I had a bunch in stock that would fit any locks like them at Hillside."

"I see." As Jackson said them, the two words had special meaning, but Long did not seem to understand, and remained as he was, looking at us hostilely.

"Did Myra have her own keys to all the doors?"

"I don't pry into folks' business. You'd naturally suppose she would, but their locks and keys never done 'em any good if someone wanted in. They wasn't worth that!"

Long snapped his fingers in illustration. "Why, I could lock up just as good in the little place I used to live."

"Where was that?"

"If you've ever been over the King place you'd know that there's a stretch of farm land of theirs from the back of the house to the river," said Long, unbending a little. "And right near the river is a farm house with trees around it. It ain't paid to cultivate the land lately; they mostly just hay it off. So things are kind of grown up, and I guess maybe some of the hoboes from the jungle come up and sleep in the house when it's stormy."

"Very likely. I remember the place now, and it's pretty well run down. By gosh!" Jackson ended suddenly. "Like as not that is where Philip King was when he first came in—down there by the jungle."

"Very likely," I agreed, before I looked at Long again— and found that Jackson had struck fire that time.

The old man was shaking and fairly convulsed with rage that seemed both pitiful and dangerous.

"Phil King—back—Phil King back!" was all he seemed able to choke out for an instant.

Then while Jackson murmured vaguely soothing words, Long raised one clenched fist toward the ceiling.

"Phil King, that I thought was dead—damn him!" he said.

But none of Jackson's questions, either commanding or coaxing, could wring any more from him than that, which he repeated over and over, quite oblivious of us.

Jackson gave it up as a bad job finally, and we left him.

"Drop me at the drugstore corner," said Jackson, yawning. "Tell White all about it, and that I'll be over first thing after I get back from Millton. I have a feeling that tomorrow we may get somewhere."

"Well, if you don't," I said, remembering a song heard over the radio, "send for our free booklet—how to detect, in ten lessons."

XX

A Shot in the Night

That ends Doug's part of the narrative. As I have said, we had dinner and then sat around and tried to kill time, waiting for him and Jackson to return. We were rather more curious than alarmed, as we could not imagine anything serious had occurred, but none of us were inclined to go to bed until one or both had come. White gave us some mild hints about needing a little rest, but all of these were blandly ignored, and he soon gave up and contented himself with a half doze in his chair.

Presently Madeline began to play the piano, with Jack standing by her, ostensibly to turn the music, though I am certain he could not read a note of it After several selections, which I enjoyed, for Madeline played well, Juliet crossed to "White and deliberately drew another chair close to his. She had been unusually silent all evening and I was not unprepared for her words.

"Mr. White, I am going to play the meddling female, and ask if you've done something—and if you haven't, if you will do it."

White had a marked fancy for Juliet, which her smile as she said this did nothing to dispel.

"I wouldn't call you meddling by any means, Miss Selby, and you've a good many brains in that little head of yours," he said gallantly. "What is it?"

"Well, have you tried to find out where Walter got that bottle of whisky?"

"Why—no," said White, surprised. "We hadn't, because we naturally figured he brought it with him."

"So did I, until I got to thinking about it," said Juliet. "Undoubtedly he brought some—quite a bit—with him, because he wouldn't be able to get that from Ellen's stock. But we all knew he was drinking a good deal Saturday, but Sunday he seemed to have stopped. Perhaps he stopped because he didn't have any more to drink."

"I see," said White. "And then he got some more—but where?"

"I don't know, but you may remember that when Jackson wanted to know where he was he couldn't find him for quite a while. He didn't say where he had been, but Myra told us he had come into the house again from the back."

"So that he might have got word to someone and stepped out to get a fresh supply?" said White. "That's fairly reasonable, Miss Selby. What do you think, Haynes?"

I was afraid when I said finally, "It certainly would bear investigation," that I had been noticeably long in answering, and added hastily, "How did you come to think of it, Juliet?"

"I was wondering, first, if an outsider might not have been responsible for Ellen's death. But if one person was responsible for both deaths, it must have been someone in the house who had an opportunity to put poison in Walter's whisky—unless he did get that bottle from someone on Sunday."

"That's true, except that Trent was in the upstairs part of the house at one time Sunday evening," said White.

"Yes, I know, but—" Juliet left her sentence unfinished, and White said again.

"But your supposition seems fairly reasonable, and I'll certainly investigate it. We've cleaned up the bootleggers in this town fairly well, but it's still possible to get the stuff, and Jackson and I know where to look. There are one or two who make a little money selling home-made poison, and they'll talk in a case like this. Have you had any other bright idea, Miss Selby?"

"Oh, I've had a number of ideas, but none of them are bright, I'm afraid," said Juliet wearily. "I'm not even sure that this one will turn out to be. What do you suppose is keeping Doug?"

"Very likely Jackson has struck soma kind of trail and they're following it up together," said White, making an excellent guess, though we did not know it at that minute. "He's nobody's fool—Jackson—and he's been nosing around for the last three days. For that matter, Martin is pretty keen himself. They're both better fitted for this work than I am, but I'll not do so very much harm as long as I realize my limitations."

Madeline had stopped playing and now she and Page joined us.

"When do we get out of here?" said Page abruptly. "This isn't doing my job any good, and none of us are helping matters along by staying."

"Oh, you might get away day after tomorrow," said White mildly. "They'll hold the inquest on Walter King tomorrow—you'll have to stay for that, and when it's over, we'll see. It's hard on all of you. Martin has a business to carry on, too."

"Of course he has, but at least he's his own boss. If I don't get away pretty soon, I won't have a job. My firm is a conservative one and doesn't care for this kind of publicity," said Page. "Besides, we aren't doing any good staying, and I, for one, want to get away as soon as possible."

"You will," said White soothingly. "I suppose they'll roast us plenty and say things about 'hick policemen,' but we've got no reason to hold you, and we won't do it any longer than is necessary."

"There is some business that hasn't been done," said Page. "Shouldn't that will have been read this afternoon? Not that it's anything to me," he added hastily. "But on Madeline's account—"

"Oh, but I don't care; there was no reason to do it," said Madeline quickly. "And with Mark so ill and Walter—"

"That's the reason Martin didn't bother about it," said White. "Everyone knows the provisions, and since Walter King is dead, that makes a difference in the will as it now stands. I suppose you realize that?" he added rather pointedly to Page.

"Certainly I do," said Page, flushing hotly, "But if you mean to imply—"

"I don't deal in implications," said White shortly. "Also Mark King is very ill, and if he dies that will change things still more."

"And if I should—die," said Madeline with a little catch in her voice, "that would be all of us. Oh, I don't know why I talk that way. It's cowardly, but sometimes I'm afraid!"

"Don't you worry," said White kindly. "I'm staying here just to prevent anything like that. And what would anyone gain? There's no—I don't know what the legal term for the thing is—"

"Residuary legatee?" I suggested. "I don't believe there is."

"Well, so there's no reason for you to be afraid, Miss West."

"I suppose not. I'll try not to be. It's just that all our nerves are on edge, staying here—and so many terrible things happening."

She did not say Walter's name, but Page looked a trifle sullen.

"I wish Doug would come," said Juliet, looking uneasily at the clock which just now struck eleven. "He drives so recklessly—perhaps they've had an accident."

"They'd have notified us long before this," said White soothingly.

But Juliet continued to be restless and uneasy, and I thought it was very hopeful for Doug's speedy success, so I was really rather sorry when he came in about fifteen minutes later.

He was dirty and heavy-eyed and he threw himself into the nearest chair with an exaggerated groan.

"Never again," he told us. "White, that constable of yours is a bloodhound. I go over to bring him back here, a matter of three miles and five minutes at the most. Here am I, five hours later, having traveled something like a hundred and fifty miles."

"But what doing?" said Juliet eagerly. "Have you discovered something? Tell us, Doug."

"Oh, we've discovered plenty," said Doug. "But nothing that helps us here, I'm afraid, though Jackson may think differently. To be brief, we've run down a long-lost uncle for you, Madeline."

"A long-lost uncle?" Madeline echoed. "Why—what do you mean?"

"For heaven's sake, tell us, Doug, and stop being mystifying," said Juliet impatiently.

"Very well, then—here's the story—"

Douglas told it as concisely as possible, but at that it took some time, as one or the other of us kept interrupting him with questions, trivial and otherwise.

Juliet was the first to break the silence that followed the ending of Doug's tale.

"Never again will I make facetious remarks about long-lost brothers," she murmured. "It does happen—they do come back."

"Of course they do, my dear—quite often," I said. "I've known more than one returned prodigal in my own experience. It's the coincidence that is startling."

"Too damn startling, if you ask me," said Page.

"Well, I shall never jeer at coincidence, either," said Juliet quickly. "But why did he come back?"

"We don't know," Douglas began.

"But Trent had his own words for it—that he came back to get what was coming to him," said Page. "It's a pretty mess. I suppose this upsets everything."

"About the will? Well, if you're worrying about that," said Douglas dryly, "I'll tell you that you'd better settle the thing out of court. It will be less expensive in the long run. He was entitled to a share under his father's will, and he has never had it. Ellen's death doesn't mean he loses those rights."

"I'm not thinking of that," said Madeline. "It's just that I can't grasp having an uncle. Aunt Ellen never spoke of him to me that I remember—except once, and then she spoke as if he were dead."

"Undoubtedly she supposed that he was," said Doug. "And everyone else must have forgotten him. I'm anxious to hear Myra's reaction to this."

"We had better tell her," said Madeline. "He will have to be brought here as soon as he can leave the hospital, you know."

She touched a bell that Ellen had used and Myra had always answered very promptly. She certainly showed no haste in obeying its summons now, but she finally appeared and stood in the doorway, regarding us unfavorably.

Madeline looked at me helplessly and I took the initiative.

"You remember when we were talking of Philip King?"

Myra's brief nod signified that she did, and her expression said plainly: "I'm not going to talk," so I abandoned any effort to lead up to my news: "Well, he's come back."

Myra was so startled that she showed it. "Come back? Merciful powers! Well," she finished, with a return to her usual stolidity, "I always said that a bad penny will turn up. Where is he?"

"He's in the hospital at Millton, but he'll want to come here when he's better," said Madeline timidly.

Myra grunted—an unlovely word, but the only fitting one for an equally unlovely sound.

"I s'pose so," she conceded. "He took his time about getting here, so I guess there's no great hurry now. What's wrong with him?"

"Well—he—that is, he is suffering from a nervous collapse—"

"In plain words, Mr. Haynes, he's been boozing too much," said Myra. "I guessed as much. Well, I'll do my best to make him comfortable for Miss Ellen's sake. She would have been glad to have him come home any time these last twenty years or more." She turned to go, then stopped with a sudden question.

"When did he get here and how did he happen to be traipsing around over at Millton?"

"Oh, he wasn't at Millton till Mr. Trent took him there," said Douglas, watching her face. "He came to Trent's Saturday night, but he must have been around here before that—perhaps a day earlier."

"A day earlier?" Myra almost drawled it, and a sort of blankness came over her face. "He come back at a—good time," she said without expression and went out.

White shook his head and muttered something about granite.

"Solid rock," Douglas agreed with a grin. "You'll have to blast to make any impression there."

"I think a little blasting, as you call it, wouldn't be a bad idea," said Page. "She knows a lot more than she wants to tell."

White looked at him with a shade of speculation in his glance, but "More than likely," he said pleasantly. "I think Jackson, has in mind to tackle her, as well as—others tomorrow. Well, since Martin is here and we've heard what he has to tell, suppose we go to bed? I'll want to be up and about early tomorrow morning."

White had his choice of Mark's, Ellen's or Walter's room, and I noticed with a little uncalled-for amusement that he chose Mark's, the least comfortable of all. We had barely all said good night in the hall when there was a light tap at our door, and Juliet presented herself, smiling, but a little pale. "I hate to disturb you so soon, but I happened to look down before I lowered the window blinds—and I'm almost certain there is a man down there, prowling around the house."

Douglas looked at me and then shrugged resignedly. "Well, Julie, so long as it's you and I know you're not a hysterical female, I'll go down and see. It may turn out to be Jackson doing some more investigating—or you may just have seen a fine, large collection of shadows."

"I hope so," said Juliet. "But I'm certain—and Doug, don't go down there by yourself. I think he has a gun; a shotgun, you know. Please get Mr. White to go with you."

"I'll be all right alone— Oh, well, if you feel that way, I'll get White," Doug yielded. "I suppose he has a gun and it might come in handy—if all he does is shoot Jackson."

White came out of Mark's room with Douglas, hastily refastening his shirt with a "what next?" expression on his face.

"Probably one of those hobos looking for something to eat," was his opinion. "Well, we'll see what we can find. Better go as quietly as we can."

In spite of their frowns and my whispered protests, Juliet crept after them down the stairs and I followed her. White opened the front door as silently as possible and the two men stepped out onto the porch.

"No one in sight," White whispered. "Suppose we go around the house in different directions and take a look. Yell if you see anyone."

In the silence that followed their going, Juliet ventured nearer and nearer to the door and finally out to the porch.

"My dear, you shouldn't come out here," I said nervously, but still keeping with her. "You're a splendid mark for a shot if anyone has tendencies that way."

"Oh, don't worry about me, Uncle Gilbert. No one is concerned with me that way. Listen—"

We heard the sound of heavy bodies colliding and someone panting incoherent words, then White's voice on the other side of the house:

"Where is he? Have you got him? I'm coming—"

Juliet was fairly dancing up and down in excitement and anxiety, and only my restraining grasp kept her on the porch.

"Oh, go on! Don't talk about it, you old idiot!" she cried with gritted teeth. "The other side—they're on the other side—"

She was cut short by the noise of a shot, and her fury left suddenly as she leaned limply back against one of the thick pillars of the porch.

"Oh—Uncle Gilbert!" she said, like a badly frightened child. "Oh, Uncle Gilbert!"

I heard them stirring to alarm upstairs and Myra's harsh voice from the hall.

"Look after Juliet," I called to her. "I'll go see, my dear—it's all right, I'm sure—"

As I ran down the steps I heard the pounding footsteps of someone in flight and White's shouted command:

"Halt or I fire!"

Then, most welcome sound of all, Doug's voice speaking to me from the shadows near the kitchen door.

"No, I'm all right. That shot was accidental, anyway. Give me a hand up—this is a damn ignominious position to be in."

"Yes, and the whole household is aroused and Juliet almost fainting on the porch," I said, rendered a trifle shrewish by my very relief.

"Well, it's worth something to have Juliet almost faint over me—though I can't imagine her doing it. She's too game for that," said Doug. "Come on—help me up."

I did as he asked, grumbling: "Can't you get up yourself—?" until I felt him wince heavily as he got to his feet. "What's the matter? You said that that shot was accidental—"

"The shot was, but the butt of his gun didn't go wild," said Douglas. "He fought like a wildcat—a whole ton of them, in fact, and in the fracas he smashed me over the arm with the end of his gun. That was when he got away."

We had reached the lighted porch by now and Juliet gave a choked cry of relief as she saw us. Madeline and Jack had come down and were standing in the doorway, Jack fully dressed and Madeline in negligee, with her dark hair hanging about her shoulders. "Someone prowling about the house," I said briefly. "Doug got mixed up with him. I think he's going to need a doctor."

"Grimley won't thank me for calling him out at twelve o'clock," said Doug. "I'd better get Page to run me over to the village."

"But where is White?" said Juliet, coming to Doug's side. "What is it, Doug? That shot—"

"No, the shot went wide. As a matter of fact, I think the gun simply went off while we were struggling. As to White, I suppose he's still chasing our friend. Good old

White, he acted in the best tradition—yelled 'Halt or I fire' before he shot."

Douglas grinned at the recollection, though his face was white and he swayed a little before Juliet unobtrusively guided him to the living-room Chesterfield.

"If he did shoot," said Juliet disgustedly. "Silly old thing, shouting to know where you were and who it was, instead of running to help you."

"He came as fast as he could, at that," Doug protested. "Served me right for thinking I could handle the whole thing by myself."

"But didn't you see who it was?" said Page.

"I couldn't see anything, but I've a pretty good idea who it was," said Doug, trying to get his arm in a less painful position. "Do you suppose you could rig up a sling of some kind, Julie? I'm pretty certain it was our friend, Jed Long."

"But why would he come here?" said Madeline as Juliet hastily seized a long, fringed piano scarf, knotted it and flung it over Doug's head. "He hasn't anything against any of us, has he?"

"You'll have to ask Mr. Long. He's supposed to have a healthy dislike for the whole King family," said Doug. He had touched rather lightly on their visit to Long. "Thanks, Juliet—stick my arm in it, will you? Easy! All right—but he may come gunning for Philip King. We unfortunately mentioned that he was back, but not that he was still in Millton, so perhaps Long thought he'd find him here."

"But even then, what had Uncle Philip done to Jed Long?" said Madeline.

"Don't know—maybe Myra can tell you, or Long may be willing to talk—" Douglas spoke jerkily, and Juliet, who had been watching him with concerned eyes, interrupted:

"Doug, you must get your arm fixed. You can't ride over to town—let me call Grimley or some other doctor at the hospital. There is one, isn't there?"

"Oh, I can manage. I'm not precisely happy, but it's a short ride. I thought we ought to wait till White came back," said Doug. "He may be needing help."

"Shall I try to locate him?" said Jack Page unenthusiastically. "If someone can find me a flashlight—" He was spared the necessity of venturing into the dark by the arrival of White, panting and generally disheveled.

"He hurt you, Martin? Got clean away, but I think I nicked him in the leg. It looked to me like Jed Long. What did he do to you?"

"Smashed my arm with his confounded gun; one of these heavy, long old hunting contraptions. It was Long, I'm pretty sure. Never had any idea the old man could be so strong."

"Well, I hope he's strong enough to get home with a bullet in his leg, because I'm going over there to his place right now, and I don't want to have to comb the surrounding country for him," said White, roused to unusual energy. "You phone the hospital, Miss Selby, and tell young Turner to come over here right away. He stays there nights. No, I'll do it myself, to be sure of getting him here. Doctors don't like to leave their beds as well as they did in the old days."

Douglas was beginning, "I could ride over," but White squelched him immediately.

"No, you couldn't. You'll stay right here. I'll phone over, and, Mr. Haynes, you take him up and get him in bed."

I could not restrain a smile at the idea of my taking Douglas anywhere, as he towers over me some five inches, but he went upstairs docilely enough, probably guessing that White would take a hand otherwise.

After a good deal of exertion on my part and some harmless swearing on Doug's, he was propped up in bed to wait for the doctor. There was a knock at the door and Juliet came in with a decanter and wine-glass.

"Myra thought Doug might have a little of this," she said, putting them on the table. "It—it's Ellen's best old port. Shall I pour you some?"

She was talking rather nervously and looking everywhere but directly at us.

"I'll take a little; glad of the excuse," said Doug, and watched her pour out the wine.

"Here—you should be flattered that Myra sent it to you," Juliet said, trying to speak lightly as she turned to hand the glass to him.

Then they both forgot Myra, myself or the famous port as they looked at each other wordlessly. Finally Douglas said huskily:

"Julie, will you—"

I went out and closed the door, though perhaps under the circumstances I should have stayed to chaperon them. But I admit that I was a little slow in drawing the door to, slow enough to hear Juliet's voice:

"Oh, yes, Doug—yes!"

XXI

A Key to the House

I had a restless night of it, for although Doctor Turner pronounced the break a simple fracture, Doug slept badly, and I was on the alert with water and cigarettes at intervals all through the night, though Doug kept telling me to "go to sleep and not bother about him."

Myra made allowances for the strain of the last day and night and did not ring the warning gong until nearly nine o'clock. Douglas struggled into his clothes with my help, and permitted me to shave him, sitting with the rigidity of a man who expects to have his throat slashed at any moment—though I only cut him once, and very slightly.

All this took time, however, and it was nearly nine-thirty before we went downstairs, to find the others already there and White just arrived.

White said that he had had breakfast but would take another cup of coffee.

"Well, I got him, all right," he said, when this was before him. "He didn't beat me home much, I guess. Anyway, I had him with the goods. My shot just nicked him, and I found him trying to stop the bleeding and do it up himself. If that wasn't enough, there was his gun, with one shot missing."

"What did he say?" I asked, watching Juliet butter biscuits for herself and Douglas and cut a strip of bacon into crisp pieces for him. "What did you do with him?"

"Hauled him off to the jail," said White. "Couldn't take any chances with his skipping out after last night. As to what he said—mighty little. Tried to tell me he'd been hunting and his gun went off and shot him. When I told him there was no use trying to put over that story, he went sullen and wouldn't talk at all. But I think he will, when we put it up to him that his actions are mighty suspicious."

"Do you mean that he might have killed Aunt Ellen?" said Madeline, her eyes widening.

"It doesn't seem quite possible with what we know just now," said White frankly. "But when we have investigated a little more we might clear up a few points that stand in the way."

Douglas shook his head. "I don't think you'll ever do it, White. There's always the question of the gun."

"Well, as Jackson has pointed out, Walter King's gun may not have been the one used, after all. We have never been able to verify the fact that the gun we found was his, you know. Of course, neither Long nor King could have been in possession of that gun."

"Where did it go to, then?" said D0ug.

White shook his head.

"We don't know, of course, unless Walter King lied, and he had reclaimed it himself but hesitated to tell us so, because it would have looked bad for him. His gun was a very common type—one that any number of people might have owned. Jackson has sent the gun and bullets to a ballistic expert, but we haven't a report, yet, and I think we'd better try to see if the gun we have was bought anywhere around here."

"Long isn't the type who would think of a silencer," said Doug.

"Now Martin," said White, with a tolerant smile, "don't go talking about people not being the type to do this or that, because you'd be surprised what they will do, sometimes."

Douglas accepted the reproof in silence, but looked unconvinced.

"But you spoke of my uncle, Mr. White," said Madeline. "Surely you don't suspect him?"

"I suspect everyone, Miss West," said White patiently. "That is, nearly everyone—and Jackson does suspect everyone. But we need to hear from your uncle himself before we go ahead on that line, and Jackson is tending to that. Now, I've got to be going, because I have a heavy morning ahead of me. I'm not sure we'll have that inquest today. Very sorry, but it doesn't look as if it would be best."

I thought Jack Page was going to burst into vehement protest, but Madeline's hand laid on his, checked anything he might have said.

"And I suppose we have to stick around here," said Douglas with a glance at his bandaged arm. "I'm afraid I'm not much use now."

"Oh, the time will pass soon enough," said White, with a benevolent glance from Douglas to Juliet that showed he understood perfectly how matters stood between them. "I'll be back later to let you know definitely about the inquest, and Jackson will probably turn up here this morning."

"We couldn't go in to see how Mark is?" said Madeline.

"I'm afraid there's not much use in your going, Miss West," said White gently. "He's just the same this morning. But I've no objections to any of you taking a ride or walk this afternoon. You've certainly been cooped up here a long time and some exercise and fresh air would do you all good."

Beyond walking about in the garden, none of us availed ourselves of White's suggestion that morning. I for one, did not care to miss Jackson, as I had an idea that he was going to conduct something of an inquisition when he came, and even if he did not, he would have news of Philip King.

I wandered about among the roses, until the hot morning sun drove me in, reflecting as I went, with an absurd feeling of injury, that now I would always be in the way with two engaged couples in the house. As a result, I gave Trent a very warm welcome when he came in about eleven o'clock.

"Jackson asked me to meet him here," Trent explained. "Hasn't he come? Well, I suppose it took him longer than he thought." He smiled rather wryly. "I suppose Douglas told you about his and Jackson's tracing of me? It was really a very creditable piece of work."

"Well, no harm will come of it," I said hastily. "You would have had to own up some time."

"Yes, I know. The harm was in trying to hide him in the first place. I have simply made Jackson view poor Philip with more suspicion because of what I did."

"But you don't think he has any really serious suspicions of King?"

"I don't know. I don't see how he can have, but," said Trent slowly, "I am sure Phil must have been thoroughly intoxicated the day before he came to me, and liquor often made him quite—irresponsible. I was sometimes called on to—well, find and bring him home, when he was a boy here, and one could never calculate exactly what effect drinking would have had on him. The fact that being in such a state he might act in a way quite impossible to him when sober is one of Jackson's points, of course."

"But the only reason he would have for killing Ellen would be because she still refused to give him his share outright," I said. "And I can't seriously imagine Ellen doing such a thing."

"Great Heavens—no! They might have disagreed later on," said Trent. "But in the moment of first meeting him Ellen would have thought only of welcoming him and would have said that certainly his share was still waiting. She wouldn't have argued about his control of money then."

"Trent," I said desperately, "can't you see light somewhere! Don't you know anything that would help us!"

Trent was silent for a moment, biting his lip under his short gray mustache.

"We've known each other a long time and we were both Ellen's friends for years," he said finally. "I ask you to believe that I know nothing more definite than you do. You thought she was worried the night you came here. I knew she had been for a number of days. When I tried to gain her confidence, she told me of her trouble with Mark and Walter, and I had to accept that as being her real reason for worry, but I always felt that there was something else which troubled her, I have felt the same thing before, though infrequently."

I had an impulse for an instant to tell Trent of what we had read in Ellen's diary, but decided that I must first consult the other members of the "partnership."

"Forgive my asking, but why wouldn't Ellen marry you?"

Trent paled a trifle, but he answered: "She said that she would be a handicap to me with her blindness. I told her that whether we married or not, there would never be any other woman for me, and there never was, so that her purpose was certainly not fulfilled. But, again, I always felt that there might be another reason, and yet I swear I do not know what it was."

"I never met her father. What sort of man was he?"

"Rather harsh—reserved and inclined to be moody, though at times he could be very charming. I admit he was not often—or to me," said Trent. "He opposed our marriage, you know. Ellen was most like him, though she resembled him only in possessing his strong will and clear head, which seemed lacking in Rose and Philip. I hardly remember their mother, but I imagine they resembled her. Sometimes I wonder," he added abruptly, "if Phil could have been in communication with her all these years, without my knowing."

"But didn't you read her letters to her?"

"Some of them, yes. Others she had Myra read; and there may have been still others that we never saw. In that case, I cannot imagine who her confidant was."

"It might be a good idea to think it over and try to fix on a possible person," I suggested. "It might turn out to be important."

"I suppose so," said Trent somberly. "But I'm about at the end of my tether, Haynes. I've thought too much."

"So have all of us," I said.

"I suppose we all have. You know Ellen had very few intimate friends, and besides Myra and myself, I can't imagine anyone to whom she would give her confidence. But wait—I had forgotten. She decided at one time to have a secretary and companion, and there was a young woman here for a short time. I don't even remember her name, because she only stayed about two weeks. Ellen had no fault to find with her, but she said she couldn't bear having someone around whom she had never seen and didn't know well."

"Was this very long ago?"

"Oh yes. It was shortly before Rose West died. Madeline was just a baby, but she hadn't come here to live yet. Myra may remember the girl's name."

Our conversation was ended by the arrival of Jackson, who had just come from Millton, he told us.

"King is much better and talks quite rationally this morning, though he is a nervous, excitable type, and I had to handle him carefully or have the nurses jumping all over me. He admitted he came into town Friday afternoon. You see, I'd checked up at the station and knew he didn't come in by train—that is, by passenger train. He says he hopped a freight with two bums, and they rolled out of it a little way from town. Then he and these two other fellows managed to get a good supply of hooch and proceeded to drink until they all passed out, according to his story. It took him most of Saturday to get sobered up enough to come around to you. He admits he hasn't much idea what was going on part of the time, but he's dead sure he wasn't away from the jungle till he came up to you. He can't give us the names of the two bums he was with—doubt if they have any—but he furnished pretty fair descriptions of them, and we may be able to pick them up and verify his story."

"Even if you do not, have you anything to hold him on?" said Trent.

"Well, perhaps not," said Jackson cautiously. "I don't intend to lose track of him, however. In the meantime, I want to see everyone who is here for a few more questions. White won't come back till afternoon, but my time is short, so we'd better get it over now. Suppose you round them up, Mr. Haynes."

I stopped to ask:

"Has White seen Long yet?"

"I believe he's spent a good deal of time with him this morning," said Jackson with a slight grin. "He said he'd tell me the results later. Too bad Martin got mixed up with the old wildcat."

Juliet, Madeline, Douglas and Jack Page came at once; Myra muttered something about lunch being spoiled, but finally put in a tardy appearance, wearing her apron as a sign of protest, I suppose. If Jackson noted it as such, he ignored it.

"The inquest had better be postponed until tomorrow," he announced. "In the meantime, I'm trying to clear up some matters before then. In the first place, we do not know that Walter King was murdered by the same person who was responsible for Miss King's death. We have to attack that problem from that viewpoint, too. First, let me ask you if any of you know of an enemy that he might have had, or did have."

Page muttered something indistinct.

"Yes, Mr. Page, what is it?"

"I only said that a good many people disliked him."

"No doubt," said Jackson blandly. "You were one of those, weren't you?"

"I didn't like him—I admit it, said Page defiantly.

"Why, if you please?"

"There's no law compelling you to like everyone you know, is there?" said Jack, "I never cared for him, but I managed to get along with him until we came here and he kept bothering Madeline and—oh well—"

He faltered and stopped under Madeline's distressed look.

"Naturally you don't like to talk about it, but I'm afraid you'll have to. You resented his attitude toward Miss West?"

"I certainly did."

"So much so that you warned him Saturday night not to continue in his actions?"

Page started.

"I did, but—"

"Yes, you were overheard," said Jackson dryly. "And he didn't pay much attention to your warning, did he?"

Page did not answer and Madeline said quickly:

"Walter didn't really mean anything, Mr. Jackson. We were fond of each other and had been together a great deal of our lives."

"But Mr. Page didn't realize that, did he?"

"No—" Madeline caught herself hastily. "Not at first, but when I kept explaining—"

"I see. You had to keep explaining?"

Madeline flushed and this time she failed to answer.

"But Walter King did want to marry you, Miss West?" Jackson asked relentlessly.

"He talked about it. I always laughed at him—I'm sure he knew it was impossible. We were cousins; besides, he knew that I didn't love him, that way."

Jackson let the matter drop and turned back to Page, but Madeline interposed courageously:

"If you're looking for motive, Mr. Jackson, I'm afraid that I—and Mark, of course—benefit by Walter's death, financially."

"Of course I realize that, Miss West," said Jackson calmly. "Even with your uncle's claims to be settled you will be very well to do. But you are well off, too, I believe, Mr. Page?"

I felt sorry for Jack, as he turned a slow red and hesitated.

"No, I'm not," he said finally. "I was pretty well fixed, but like a lot of other fools I thought I could beat the market and they took me to the cleaners. That's one reason I'm very anxious to keep my job, and this isn't helping me."

"I understand that," Jackson agreed politely. "And I'm very sorry. But you see, Mr. Page, to put it bluntly, you are also going to benefit by these deaths."

"No, I don't see," said Page, controlling himself with an obvious effort. "Because I am not going to marry Madeline until I can offer her something more than my present salary."

"I see," said Jackson, with such an open lack of belief that Page flushed again, angrily. "Do you drink, Mr. Page?"

"As much and no more than the average man," Page snapped. "If you mean, am I an habitual booze-hound—no!"

"I didn't suppose so. But you do carry liquor with you at times, don't you?"

"No—that is, very seldom," said Page, after a barely perceptible pause.

"You didn't bring any with you on this visit?"

"No. I sometimes carry a flask when I am invited to a party or dance."

"I see," said Jackson, again. "And you did not— What is it, Miss Bell?"

"He brought a bottle with him when he come," said Myra dispassionately. "I saw it in his room."

"Yes? What kind of a bottle, please?"

"They all look about the same to me," said Myra. "This wasn't very big, and it was flat. That's all I can tell you. He kept it in his bureau drawer."

"You had no right to pry into the things in anyone's room," said Madeline indignantly.

Myra glanced at Madeline, unimpressed.

"It was my work to clean up the bedrooms, an' when a man leaves dirty collars an' handkerchiefs all over the bureau, I put them in a drawer. He wasn't making no effort to hide this; it was in plain sight."

"Is it still there?"

"I couldn't say, not having had time to do much more than make up beds lately."

"No, it isn't there now," said Page.

"Oh—well, I am rather curious to know what you did with the bottle when you were through with it," said Jackson.

"I didn't drink the stuff. I don't know. It disappeared from my room," said Page desperately.

"It disappeared? When?"

"Sometime Friday. At least, it was there Friday morning, but not at night when I went to bed."

"And you have no idea where it went?"

"I thought then that Mark had taken it. He was planning to go out that night, and he was grumbling because the flask he carried was empty and he didn't have much money. He knew I had this."

"I see." Jackson's reiteration of those two words was beginning to grate on me, and they obviously rasped Page's already unsteady nerves. "Did Walter King ask you for anything to drink, by any chance?"

Madeline caught her breath, but Page only looked at the constable dully.

"No—no, he didn't," he said. "He had plenty of his own; He had at least two bottles like the one I brought."

Jackson forbore to say "I see" this time, but there was no doubt that he did see the significance of Page's unfortunate admission.

"I won't ask you and Miss Selby to go over your actions on the night of the first murder again, Miss West," he went on. "Now Martin—when the alarm had been given, I think you said you and Mr. Haynes came out into the hall, which was dark?"

"Yes," said Douglas. "We naturally hesitated an instant and then the lights were flashed on by Walter King, and I ran forward. By that time Page had joined us."

"Very well. Now, Mr. Page, on the afternoon of the next day, when the cook raised the disturbance that led to discovering Mark King, where were you?"

"Upstairs—wasn't I? I came down just as everyone was gathered around Annie, trying to find out what was wrong," said Page wearily. I imagine he may have begun to feel some belated sympathy for Walter under Jackson's persistent questioning.

"Why had you gone upstairs?"

"My God—I don't know! Why shouldn't I go up to my room if I wanted to? It was supposed to be a free house, not a jail!"

"I thought you might remember," said Jackson. "Now, that same night when the tapping occurred—all of you knew you were locked in?" This question was the merest formality to all but Page and he recognized the fact by answering:

"Certainly I knew I was locked in. I had time to try the door before it was unlocked."

"A key was on the outside of the door, however?"

"Yes—" Page saw the trap and amended his answer hastily, "that was what Martin said."

"I believe that is all along that line," said Jackson unexpectedly. "There is no point in my asking any of your actions on the day before or the night before Walter King was murdered, as it is impossible to narrow down the time at which the poison was put in the bottle. Besides," he added casually, "he may have received it already poisoned. Now, a few questions to you, Miss Bell?"

Myra looked, at him scornfully for an instant, but made no other protest.

"I believe you did not hear anything of importance on the night of Miss King's murder and did not know that she was dead until Mr. White told you?" Myra nodded. "Yet we know that someone entered the cellar and burned papers and struck down Mark King—and yet you heard nothing."

"We ain't right over the cellar," said Myra briefly. "And me and Annie are a little hard of hearing."

"I hadn't noticed that in you. It seems to me that you hear very well," said Jackson. Myra was silent; her unresponsiveness to anything but a direct question—

and sometimes to that—was a splendid defense against cross-examination. "Do you know if Mark King was in the habit of entering the house by the back door?"

"When he was out too late he did. He had a key to the kitchen door, and we never left any key in the front door or the back one either, so's he could get in all right. I knew he did it, but there was no use bothering Miss Ellen any more by telling her."

"Where were you when Annie began to scream that afternoon?"

"In the garden getting flowers for the table."

"Did anyone see you?"

"I couldn't say," said Myra indifferently. "If they looked out the windows, they would have easily enough." But none of us was able to answer the interrogative glance Jackson sent each in turn.

"Do you know if Walter King had whisky in his room Sunday morning?"

"I told you I was too busy to give the upstairs rooms more than a lick and promise."

Jackson tried another tack. "You had been with Miss King a number of years. Were she and her brother on good terms before he left?"

"I guess you know he left in a huff over their father's will. Up to that time they always was."

"Do you know of any other reason he might have remained away from home for so long?"

"No." Myra folded her lips tightly and then apparently changed her mind. "It might have been on account of Jed Long threatening to shoot him because he said Mr. Philip had ruined his daughter."

"Oh—Long said that, did he? King must have thought he meant it."

"I guess he did mean it," said Myra grimly. "She wasn't worth much, but after Mr. Philip didn't come back, she did settle down and never seemed to have much joy in life after that; so Jed, he got more bitter all the time, and finally he pestered Miss Ellen about it, and she had to tell him to leave. That was the first she knew anything about it."

"Aside from him you know of no real enemies that Miss King could have had?"

Myra did not repeat her former tirade against Ellen's nearest relations—I suppose only Madeline being there would have prevented her had she been inclined to do so.

"I don't know of any," she said.

"Do you know Jed Long?" said Jackson—an apparently random question. Again Myra folded her lips and then decided, after all, to speak.

"We're second cousins, but we never had much to do with each other."

"Do you ever visit him or see him anywhere?"

"I ain't been in his house for five years; not since one time I went down there to have a key made," said Myra.

Jackson grasped at this eagerly.

"Oh, yes. Then he could have had keys that would fit this house?"

"A dozen, so far's I know. All the keys we use here are common, ordinary ones like lots of folks would have. Miss Ellen was always going to put in them Yale locks, but she never got around to it."

"Do you know of anyone else who had keys to this house?" said Jackson.

For the first time Myra's poise deserted her. She wet her lips as if they were suddenly dry.

"I don't know—people might have had keys that would fit without us knowing—"

"But I am asking if you know of any particular person who did have," said Jackson. "You have someone in mind?"

Myra shook her head mechanically.

"No—no—"

Her lowered eyes slipped around our circle furtively. Then Trent, who had grown pale, spoke:

"You had as well tell them, Myra, since you know. I have had a key to this house for nearly twenty years."

XXII

Mrs. French

After an instant of silence, Jackson said stolidly:

"You should have told us before, Mr. Trent. May I ask how you came to have the key?"

Trent went from white to red.

"I supposed the implication was sufficiently plain without my putting it into words. I had the key in order that I might—visit—Miss King."

Madeline was staring at him with unbelieving eyes; I suppose we all shared her feeling. Trent drew a deep breath.

"Perhaps you see why I didn't care to speak of it!"

Jackson also had reddened, and he looked slightly uncomfortable.

"I see, Mr. Trent. I—I believe that is all just now. If I think of anything else I will ask you individually."

Myra got up and went out of the room; Juliet, with an indignant glance toward Jackson, followed her. For an instant longer Madeline sat there, staring at the carpet, then after a murmured word to Jack, they left us also. Trent, who had been standing at a window, back to the room, turned and faced us.

"I suppose you think I am always concealing something from you, Jackson, so I am going to tell this without being asked. The conversation that was overheard between Walter and Page was not the only one that they had on the subject.

I interrupted one on Thursday evening that had evidently been rather bitter, though I heard only a few words, and of those I only recall Page's saying 'I've warned you.'"

"Thank you, Trent. I guess," said Jackson with rather overdone carelessness, "I'd better be going."

Trent had turned away again and Douglas and I were left to regard his correctly tailored back in uncomfortable restraint. Then Doug muttered something about being thirsty and got himself out of the room.

"It doesn't matter what you think about me," said Trent abruptly, without facing me. "If it doesn't make you think poorly of Ellen. For some reason she wouldn't marry me— she said she wouldn't tie me to her, but we had a few moments of happiness and I was only too grateful for that, whatever the world may say."

I cleared my throat awkwardly.

"I still think Ellen was one of the finest women I knew," was the best I could do.

It seemed to satisfy Trent; he stood there a few minutes longer, then said good morning with a fair assumption of nonchalance and started home. Presently Juliet's head appeared in the door, and then she came in with Doug.

"Myra feels dreadfully for having let this be known," she said without preamble. "She says she never blamed Ellen; she was glad to see her be happy, so she pretended she didn't know anything. She just worried for fear it would become known to others and they would speak lightly of Ellen. Just let them try—around me!" said Juliet with a dangerous glint in her eyes.

"She felt she couldn't marry him, but at least she had the courage to take what happiness she could for both of them. I suppose, though," she added soberly, "that it must often have distressed her terribly and that she wasn't happy after all."

"I'm afraid you and Myra might be accused of lacking a strict moral sense, Juliet," I said. "And I would probably be put in the same category."

"Go ahead and tell us what you said you had to tell," said Douglas, glad to divert the talk to other channels.

"Oh— Well, Myra talked more freely than she ever has, and she said that the fact that Mr. Trent had a key to the house had worried her, as well as something else. She overheard a little of their talk while we were all outside Friday night. That is, she thought by the tones of their voices that Ellen was telling him something and that they didn't agree with her. All she actually heard was Mr. Trent saying: 'If you do, you will regret it—' Myra said he spoke as if giving a warning. That may be her imagination, and it may mean nothing at all."

"Except that she may have been telling Trent about that will, and yet he won't tell us what she said," Doug suggested. "Oh, Lord—what a mess."

"Then there was one more thing," Juliet said hesitantly. "Myra was talking about Mr. Trent's devotion to Ellen and she said: 'Even that little cat of a Mrs. French couldn't get him away, though she'll try harder than ever now.' It seems that Mrs. French is a widow; one of the leaders in the town, and Mr. Trent has been more friendly with her than with anyone for years."

"Then, he might have asked Ellen for a release?" said Douglas slowly.

"She wouldn't have refused it," Juliet cried. "She would have let him go."

"Knowing Ellen, one would have supposed so," I said. "But—I'm wondering, now, did we ever, any of us, really know Ellen?"

"Apparently not," said Douglas. "In the meantime, Jackson certainly gave it to Page hot and heavy."

"He didn't come out any too well, either," said Juliet. "Especially when you consider Walter's death, and the bottle of whisky—which he admits was just like his."

"Yes, but Mark might very well have taken it, as he suggested," I said. "It would be rather like Mark. That's another thing he could clear up for us."

"Could, but probably never will," said Doug soberly. "White told me that Grimley is afraid he won't last the day out. He didn't want to say so before Madeline. Well, if Page had anything to do with this, Madeline at least, is sure of his innocence."

Juliet shook her head.

"I wouldn't be certain of that. I think she'd stick to him even if she thought he was guilty. You know, we don't know if Ellen approved of their engagement. She never mentioned it. If she didn't, that, combined with the need for money, would make a very satisfactory motive. But— call me catty, if you like—I'd be inclined to think in that case that Madeline was certainly the influence that drove him to it."

"I don't call that catty. It's perfectly possible," said Douglas. "But I would think, then, that he alone was responsible for Walter's death. I can't imagine Madeline wanting to get him out of the way. Oh, hell! Excuse me, but it makes me kind of sick, sitting here and supposing unspeakable things of people like that."

"Yes, it does," Juliet agreed. "But they may very well be doing the same by us. And I, for one, am not satisfied to ignore what Myra told me about Mr. Trent's warning to Ellen, and about Mrs. French. I am going to take Doug in to the doctor after lunch, and I am going to see Mrs. French."

"My dear—" I began.

"And I want you to go with me, Uncle Gilbert. Oh, yes, I must have you. You can be so charming and you are the very person to take along when interviewing a coquettish widow."

"But you have no right to interview her at all," I protested weakly, knowing very well that I would do what Juliet asked, in the end.

"I will say I represent a newspaper," said Juliet "I don't think she knows me, and you can be my social sponsor. She probably has heard all about you, or seen you. From what Myra told me about her, I imagine she would jump it the chance of newspaper publicity, and being considered one of Ellen's associates. You watch me! I haven't interviewed a few celebrities for nothing."

"She's going to make a peach of a lawyer's wife, isn't she?" said Douglas. Juliet frowned at him, and he went on: "I suppose you're trying to establish a motive for Trent?"

"We've always said it couldn't be done. I'm curious to see if it can," said Juliet. "We have motives for everyone but him; we might as well make a clean sweep of it."

"No, Myra is still exempt," I said. "And I think it would tax your ingenuity to discover one in that case."

"Twenty thousand dollars has been ample motive for murder many times before this," Doug said cynically. "Well, one or two more suspects and we should be perfectly happy."

Immediately after lunch Juliet drove Doug into town and I made an unwilling third to the party. We left Doug at the hospital, and turned back to Elm street, where the oldest and most well-to-do families live, and which is so named, I suppose, because it is lined with maples.

I knocked, after a last futile protest, and a maid admitted us. Mrs. French kept us waiting fifteen minutes before she came; a little, vivacious woman with persistently yellow hair. She was dressed in purple; royal purple, I believe it is called—a shade which I have never seen anyone wear satisfactorily. She was no exception. At Juliet's prompting

look, I introduced myself, and her as a "young friend connected with a city paper." Mrs. French acknowledged the
introduction very graciously, not to say gushingly.

"I have never *met* you, Mr. Haynes, but I have *heard*
so much of you from *poor* Miss King and Edward—Mr.
Trent, you know." It is needless to remark that she talked
in italics.

"And so you are a *newspaper*, woman, Miss Selby? I can
hardly *believe* it; you look so *young* and—er—innocent.
But it must be very *fascinating* work, I am sure."

"It is, and I am trying so hard to get ahead," said Juliet
appealingly. "That is why I coaxed Mr. Haynes to bring
me to see you. I thought if I could write something new
when I get back to the city, it would help me with the edi-
tor. The police don't seem to be getting anywhere at all."

"That is *just* what I have been saying. Mr. White is a
lovely man, but of course he isn't at all *fitted* for this work,
and the constable, Jackson, is really *quite* impossible. I
have thought a lot about it, myself—women are so don't
you think, Mr. Haynes?"

"I'm sure they are," I said politely, before she hurried on:

"But they are doing their *best,* of course, poor things,
though I can't help thinking this will never be *solved.* Perhaps that handsome young King had *something* to do with
it, after all, and they are mistaken when they say he was
murdered. Do you think so?"

"It's very possible," said Juliet mendaciously. "But you
have lived here for some time, Mrs. French, and of course
know everyone, and that is why I thought you might be
able to give me some sidelights on the affair."

"Me? Oh, I'm *afraid* not. I was too *young* to know Miss
King when she was a girl, of *course.* I have only been ac-
quainted with her since I moved back here. She was *charming;* we enjoyed each other's company so much. I can't

imagine anyone doing such a *cruel* thing; I can't see any *reason* for it, can you? Of course she was always a little *reserved,* but that's not important, I know."

"She and Mr. Trent were very old friends," said Juliet casually.

Mrs. French bridled slightly at this. "Oh, yes, I *believe* they were. He always looked upon her as an *older* sister, I know. Don't you think so, Mr. Haynes?"

"I—I believe so," I said lamely, thinking in how many ways she differed from Ellen. I mentally calculated her age and placed her at forty at a charitable guess, as Juliet said:

"Mr. Trent is a charming man."

"Oh, very. Really an *unusual* man. I should have been so *lonely* without him," said Mrs. French pathetically. Juliet's smile was a marvel of polite sympathy.

"I have heard him speak of you. I am sure he returns the compliment, Mrs. French."

"Oh, *thank* you. I *hope* so. In fact—" Mrs. French smiled archly. "While we are not *saying* anything yet— Well, I am sure you *understand.*"

Juliet had been going warily, but having what she wanted, she abruptly abandoned finesse.

"You mean you are going to marry Mr. Trent?"

"Oh—my dear!" Mrs. French was shocked. "We are *very* good *friends,* but you understand— While he is still involved in this *sad* business, naturally he does not want to drag *me* into it by linking our *names.* But afterward— it will be made *public.* I would be willing, now, but Mr. Trent is the *soul* of chivalry, you know."

"Oh, yes," said Juliet perfunctorily. "I'm sure he is, but I thought perhaps he had other reasons for not wanting to talk yet."

"I'm afraid I don't know what you mean," said Mrs. French, her coyness vanishing abruptly.

"Oh, I'm so sorry. I'm afraid I shouldn't have spoken of it. You didn't know that Mr. Trent might have other claims on him?"

"Certainly not. I have no idea what you mean," said Mrs. French harshly, her rouge showing in two ugly spots on her cheek bones. "If you mean Miss King—" She stopped, seeing her error.

"Then you did think of Miss King, after all?"

Mrs. French rose abruptly, half a dozen chains and bracelets jangling with the movement.

"I will not be insulted in my own home, Miss Selby! How dare you ask me such questions?"

"They are very interesting questions, to me, and perhaps to others," said Juliet, unperturbed. I, the innocent bystander, was by far the most uncomfortable of the three. "However, I suppose I have seemed rather impertinent, so perhaps I had better go. I have been very much interested in what you've told me."

Mrs. French twined her fingers about one of the dangling necklaces. She was not so stupid, after all, "I see," she said in a strained voice. "I shall tell Mr. Trent—"

Juliet looked rather disturbed for the first time.

"I suppose you will. However, there's no need of it. I shan't print anything, and I'm not connected with the police, if that is what you're afraid of."

A faint look of relief passed over the other woman's face, but she refused to be placated.

"Yes, Miss Selby, I think you are *impertinent*—decidedly so. And I am sure that when you think it *over* you will see how very *foolish* all your questions have been. Simply a *waste* of time—"

"Oh, I don't think that," said Juliet, and with that parting shot, led the way to the car.

I was perspiring freely when I got in beside her.

"There are some things one should not ask, even in the name of friendship," I told her firmly. "This is the first and last time you will ever take me on a mission of that kind."

"I hope so," said Juliet, shifting gears. "Horrid old cat! I hope I did scare her plenty. Imagine a man falling for her! But I suppose she's always very sweet—to men. She probably feeds him a lot of soft soap and makes him think he's *wonderful*. Ellen would never have done that. Perhaps that's why he likes it now."

"Well, you got what you came for," I remarked.

"Yes, and now I wish I hadn't. I'm always that way," said Juliet. "I rush ahead like this and find out things, and then I'm sorry. But I never really thought— Anyway, I'm not going to tell anyone but Doug. Don't say it's my duty to—"

"I haven't—"

"But it's on the tip of your tongue," said Juliet unreasonably. "And I don't care! I'm sure Ellen would have let him go without any fuss. I'm sure of it!"

"The lady doth protest too much," I murmured.

Juliet looked at me indignantly and drew up before the hospital where Douglas was waiting on the steps with the sheriff. I thought White looked at us rather sharply, but otherwise his manner was quite as usual.

"I came in again to see how young King is. Just the same, they say." White sighed: "They're working hard to pull him through, though Grimley says he's not sure it's a kindness to do it. I've got to have a bite of lunch now, and get busy on another line. I've been pounding away at old Long most of the morning." He grinned a trifle sheepishly. "Talk about hard nuts to crack! I wished I had some of the city Strong arm gang here several times, but he finally loosened up a little."

"What did he—" Juliet began.

"Get Martin to tell you. We've been talking about it while we were waiting for you. We had a bit of luck, too—rounded up one of the hoboes who was with Philip King. At least, he swears he was, and except for his being too drunk at the time to know much, I guess we'll have to take his word. I'll be out to the house sometime this evening, probably, and you can tell the others that we'll have the inquest tomorrow—sure."

"Did he know where we were!" Juliet demanded, as soon as we were under way again.

"I don't know. He may have. I told him I thought you were getting ice cream at the drug store but he may have known you weren't there," said Doug. "Well?"

"Well enough," said Juliet. "The lady talked. She's a gushing little peroxide blonde, but she says they're going to announce their engagement when this is over. She was very anxious for us to understand that Ellen was an older sister to Mr. Trent, but she slipped up and gave it away that she realized Ellen stood in her way."

"Just how much do you make out of it?"

"I don't know—yet. I'm not telling anyone else about this until I decide," said Juliet. "I'm not so sure—being a woman—that the so-called engagement isn't mostly of her making. Now, you tell us what you know."

"About Long, you mean? Oh, it's nothing more than I guessed," said Doug, wincing as we slid over a bump. "He finally admitted that he came gunning for Philip Bang. If we had only mentioned that King wasn't here it would never have happened. Though, in his state of mind, I wouldn't put it past him to have started out for Millton. White said he talked a good deal like the father in an old-fashioned melodrama, but that he was pretty impressive, at that. He blames King for 'ruining' his daughter, and I guess he's brooded over it until he's a little off on that subject. But he still insists that he never came near Ellen after he was told to leave the estate and I believe him."

"Yes, I think I do, too. I don't see how they could pin anything on him unless they know more than we do."

I listened to their talk rather stupidly, my main desire being for a nap. When we were back again I started up-stairs at once, but was delayed for a few minutes by Madeline, who stopped me. She looked pale and worried; her first words confirmed my impression.

"Please tell me—do you think Jack is in any danger! I am so frightened, after the way Mr. Jackson talked."

"Oh, I don't think you need worry," I said, as cheerfully as possible. "They won't do anything hastily."

"It's nothing but circumstance, and false," said Madeline, flushing momentarily. "Why, he couldn't—Jack couldn't have done it! And if even a breath of suspicion got out, it would ruin him with his firm. He is worried about that, too. It isn't fair! There are others—Myra, Uncle Edward, that old Long—even Uncle Philip. If the inquest was only over! I am so afraid of what they may say or do."

"Don't worry, an inquest never amounts to anything and you know White won't do anything rash," I repeated. "Where is Jack?"

"He's out on the porch. I just left him."

"Well, you go back and cheer him up," I advised. "And then I'd lie down a while, if I were you. You look tired out."

Madeline smiled faintly.

"Oh, I am—we all are. Thank you, Mr. Haynes."

It took me a little longer to get to sleep than I had anticipated, as something I had been turning over in my mind since the night before persisted in recurring now. In view of all we had learned that morning, I wondered if I should speak, but, I argued, Juliet and Douglas knew as much as I did and had apparently not seen any new significance in the incident.

I decided, as I dropped off to sleep, that I would continue silent, but when I woke, a good deal rested, I could not be entirely certain that my decision was justified.

Evidently Madeline had taken my advice; she was not in the living room as I went through. I found Juliet alone in the library, several closely written sheets of paper on the table before her. She covered these with one hand, flushing a little.

"At it again," she confessed. "Doug and I have talked and talked till we're in a worse muddle than ever, and I made him go out to the porch to lie down. His arm was hurting, though he wouldn't admit it."

"You modern lovers!" I said, shaking my head. "Just engaged, and you spent the afternoon trying to solve a crime."

Juliet smiled demurely.

"Oh, we talked about other things, too," she said. "But somehow we couldn't keep from thinking of Ellen, even then. She would have been glad, and because of her we have a wonderful nest egg to start on. So we always came back to it. You've seen this, haven't you?"

She showed me a tracing of the two scraps of paper, we had found in the cellar.

"I've been puzzling over it, and I just wondered—did anyone show this to Myra?"

"I don't believe so. I don't know why. Perhaps it didn't occur to them, or they thought it would be of no use. I don't believe White thought it was important."

Yet it was important; the key that would unlock the mystery to us, and that sooner than we thought. Juliet continued to pore it for a few minutes in silence.

"I think I'll show it to Myra myself," she said, but she made no immediate move toward the kitchen. "Doug and

I were listing all the facts that seem to point suspicion toward different people, and it looks worst for Jack."

"I suppose it does. Madeline is badly frightened, yet they have nothing definite against him so far as Ellen's death is concerned. And they don't know about Mrs. French, or—"

"Or what?" Juliet caught me up instantly.

"I've been thinking about it a good deal—I wonder that you and Doug haven't. You remember the conversation I told you of, that Walter and Trent had? Walter asked him to do something for him that Trent didn't want to do. Trent said Walter was doing himself no good, you remember, but he finally gave in. It has occurred to me that if Walter got that whisky from somewhere outside the house—"

Juliet stared at me.

"He made Mr. Trent get it for him! Of course—we were stupid not to have thought of that."

"Well, you two didn't hear them, and what little I told you naturally didn't make a great impression on you."

"But if—just for the purposes of argument—if Mr. Trent did get that whisky for Walter, and it was poisoned then—" Juliet stopped. "Oh, it seems impossible! Walter must have known something—"

"It certainly seems likely."

Juliet sat an instant longer, staring at the floor, and then rose, abruptly. "I'm going in to talk to Myra. I'll be back."

But she was gone so long that I grew vaguely uneasy and went to look for her. There was no sign of Myra in the kitchen, and Juliet was not in the living room with Madeline and Jack or with Douglas on the porch. A car stopped before the house, and I saw Trent coming up the path with a bundle of mail and newspapers, but I left someone else to admit him and went upstairs and knocked on Juliet's door.

"Who is it?" said Juliet's voice on the other side. "Uncle Gilbert? No, I'm all right—that is—please tell the others I have a headache if I'm not down. I've—oh, I've got to be alone for a little while, Uncle Gilbert, please! I've got to think—"

XXIII

The Riddle Answered

Sorely puzzled and debating whether to tell Douglas, I went downstairs again. Madeline had been sorting the mail and gave me my share—several bills forwarded to me. She was doing her best to overcome a slight constraint of manner toward Trent, who took Doug's letters from her and passed them to him through the window. Page was reading a typewritten communication with a worried frown; I could see the large letterhead through the paper.

"There's only one for Juliet—"

"She's lying down with a headache," I interrupted Madeline hastily. "She'll be down when it's better."

"Oh, I'm sorry. I feel much better after taking your advice."

Madeline glanced through her own mail hastily, her mind plainly with Page and the letter he was still studying.

"Thank you for bringing this—Uncle Edward."

Trent's answer was lost in the sound of another car stopping and heavy footsteps on the porch. I went to open the front door, but Jackson and White, dirty and hot, were in the hall as soon as I was.

"Everybody here?" said Jackson at once. "Is Trent here? If he isn't, we'll—" He left the sentence unfinished.

"Yes, he's here; he just came with our mail," I said uneasily. "I suppose Myra is around somewhere and Miss Selby is lying down."

"No particular use of disturbing her, unless you think she wants to be in on everything," said Jackson with a certain grimness that was not reassuring. "I'd like to have Myra in, though. I'll go find her."

"What is it?" I said, following White into the living-room. "Have you—"

"I've been digging around and I've found—plenty," said White. "I don't like it, Mr. Haynes, but we seem pretty close to knowing something at last."

"Oh," I said inadequately, and felt that inglorious empty feeling in my stomach which accompanies nervousness and dread.

Douglas looked at me from the porch, his eyebrows raised in question, and when I nodded, got up quietly and stepped through the long window into the room. Jackson came back with Myra almost at once; she looked frightened—a strange thing for Myra—and her face was haggard.

"She knows something," I kept telling myself nervously. "Perhaps in a few minutes it will be all over—in a few minutes—"

But Jackson left me little time for discussion as he took charge in that disconcertingly businesslike manner.

"I want all of you to think back to Sunday afternoon," he said. "It was Sunday night, you should remember, that Walter King was poisoned. I came in and was alarmed because I couldn't find him, but he came back and said he had been outside for a few minutes. Did anyone see him go, or where he went?"

"He passed through this room. Mr. Page and I were here," said Madeline after an instant of hesitation. "He went toward the back of the house."

"You did not see him come back? No? That's what I thought. But *you* did." He turned to Myra.

"Yes, he came back in through the kitchen and up the back stairs. I told you that," said Myra tonelessly.

"Did he—was he carrying anything?"

"I—I didn't see it if he was."

I thought she was lying; that Jackson agreed with me was evident by his sharp:

"Are you sure of that? I'm not going to have any more nonsense about this. Was he carrying anything?"

"It looked like he had a kind of a flat bottle in his pocket," Myra muttered. "It was hot to be wearing a coat, and I wondered what he was up to, anyway."

"All right; that's enough. Mr. Trent was not here then?"

"You know that as well as we do," said Doug, as no one else seemed inclined to answer. "You were here when he came."

Jackson dropped his pretense of ignorance on that point.

"Yes, I was here. Mr. Trent, you arrived soon, very soon after we had located King. Yet you left the village nearly an hour before. How do you account for that?"

"Do I have to account for it?" said Trent slowly.

"I think you'll find that you do." Jackson's tone was definitely menacing now. "When I tell you that Gladden, one of our still surviving bootleggers, remembers distinctly selling you a flat pint bottle of whisky that afternoon. He had reason to remember, because you had never been in his place before, or dealt with him in any way."

"That is true; I hadn't," said Trent.

In spite of his unmoved tone his face had gone pale. I heard a slight sound, and turned to see Juliet standing in the doorway. Jackson gave her a perfunctory glance as she took the chair nearest Doug's.

"But you found it necessary to go, that day," he said. "There's no use stalling, Trent. I showed him the bottle from which Walter King drank, and he is willing to swear that it came from his stock."

"Mightn't a person of his type be willing to swear to almost anything?" said Trent. "Oh, I'm not blaming you,

Jackson. It's evidence of the strongest kind. And Mr. Haynes probably overheard Walter's request to me—"

"He hasn't told me of it, if he did," said Jackson, with a sharp glance at me.

"No? Well, he would probably feel it necessary to tell now," said Trent. "I got the whisky for Walter, he insisted that he must have it or go crazy, and he couldn't get it himself under the circumstances. I met him in the stretch of woods back of the house."

"You suffer from insomnia at times, don't you, Mr. Trent?" said Jackson. His punctilious use of the formal title, small a thing as it was to notice, grated on me.

"I don't know what you mean," said Trent.

"I'll tell you, then. Dr. Grimley prescribed some very strong sleeping powders for you quite a while ago because you were suffering from bad headaches and quite unable to sleep, he said. You had the prescription filled here, once. The druggist remembered that, and they very much resembled the powders that were substituted for Mark King's harmless medicine. Do you happen to have any of those powders with you now?"

"I—no—I haven't used them for some time."

"Not even with all this trouble to keep you from sleeping?" said Jackson mercilessly.

"I had—some," said Trent, biting his under lip nervously. "I gave them to Ellen because she was not sleeping well. She asked me—" He came to a stop, then: "Well, I see how it is," he said, with a forced smile. "Do what you think best. If you want me to come with you— But just out of curiosity, what motive do you offer?"

"Walter King knew too much," said Jackson softly. "The letter he started to write proves that. I don't know what he saw, or how, but you're a well-to-do man, and he wanted money, so he could take a chance. For the rest, I suppose you know Mrs. French?"

Trent reddened angrily.

"Certainly I know Mrs. French. And what has she to do with this?"

"Something," Jackson did not look at Juliet or me, "something put me wise to her. It seems you are to be married, now that there are no obstacles—"

"That is a lie!" Trent's heretofore unfailing courtesy vanished suddenly. "I had no intention of marrying her! I knew her husband; she consulted me about investments. If there is an engagement, it exists only in her own mind!"

"She has given it some thought," said Jackson dryly. "Enough to know that Miss King stood in your—her way. She is jealous; if Miss King had chosen to tell you what stood—between you—"

"Miss King would not—"

Jackson paid him no attention.

"Myra, did Mr. Trent and Miss King agree about Mrs. French?"

Myra was silent. Then:

"Miss Ellen didn't like her," she admitted. All the fight seemed to have gone out of her. "I never knew them disagree but once; I heard him tell her that she'd be sorry if she did something—I don't know what."

"Perhaps you can explain those words, or would like to," said Jackson.

"No—I—can't explain them," said Trent slowly. "Oh, why keep this up! I don't have to talk; you haven't warned me that anything I say will be used against me, but you should have."

"Yes, I guess I should," said Jackson. "We haven't any option but to hold you, on Gladden's evidence alone. I guess you all see that."

Douglas was first to speak.

"It's strong enough evidence, as far as it goes. But there are still a number of things not cleared up. Are you suggesting that Mr. Trent was responsible for that tapping episode?"

"Well, why not? You admit, Mr. Trent, that you were around here Saturday night. We know you were and you had a key. Philip King is quite unable to say if you were here before him or came after him."

Trent merely wet his dry lips and looked at Jackson dully.

"Miss West—" Madeline started, and looked at him fearfully. "It seems to me that—even in the dark—you should have some idea of who your assailant was."

"I—except that it was a man—it was very dark and he came at me so unexpectedly," Madeline stammered. "I don't know—"

"Don't you think that you were rather brave to have ventured out into the hall, unless you knew who was there?" said Jackson. "You wouldn't be afraid of Mr. Trent, would you?" Madeline was silent. "Could you tell us at least in what direction he went?"

"No—no—I was unconscious—"

"But the back stairway was always handy while Sheriff White was coming up the front one," Jackson pointed out unnecessarily. "No, I think we needn't go any farther—"

"Just one instant, please." It was Juliet's voice. "I want to ask one question. You have the report of the fingerprint expert; you told us about it, but I can't recall that you ever mentioned— Were there fingerprints on Ellen's cane?"

The two officers stared at her; then, with an indulgent look, White took a sheaf of papers from his pockets and thumbed them over.

"No, according to Gray's report, there were no prints on her cane."

But Jackson, quicker in his perceptions, looked at Juliet again, with something like admiration, and frowned. "That's funny—that's damn funny—"

"It isn't right," said Douglas with sudden excitement. "Why should she bother to destroy the prints on her cane—if she used it."

"That is it—if she used it," said Juliet steadily. "We wondered why she went downstairs that night, and decided that it was to get a book. But she didn't read the book, and she left it open on the table's edge—"

"I don't see—" White began.

"But you don't know Ellen, or you would. She always closed books and put them back in place when she wasn't reading them. And she wasn't reading that night, because she was crocheting when it happened. And she wouldn't necessarily have used her cane to go downstairs. She didn't use it a great deal even for that. Myra said so herself, and we all know it."

"Then what are you trying to say, Miss Selby?" said White, getting slowly up from his chair.

"That we—Miss West and I—led you astray, as we were meant to do. That it wasn't Ellen who went downstairs; that she was probably dead then!"

"But you saw—"

"Yes, Mr. White, I saw someone. An indistinct figure, a dark kimono— It might have been a man or woman, with that silk head band to hide the hair. We've never accounted for the footsteps Uncle Gilbert heard going down the back stairs and we thought Ellen was still alive then, at one o'clock. But I think that she was dead and that was her murderer he heard."

"There's another thing," said Douglas. "Mark started home well before one, according to his friends. What would delay him until after one thirty—nearly two? But if he came home in the usual time that it would take—"

"He would be here around one," said Jackson. "Miss Selby, and you, Miss West—is there anything more that you can think of? If you are right, and we have had the murder fixed at the wrong time all along— Are you sure you don't know, or haven't some idea who it was you saw? Or did you—" He risked Doug's angry glance, "Did you see anyone?"

Juliet's eyes met his steadily.

"I saw someone, Mr. Jackson. Oh—I don't like this! But I must say it, mustn't I? Walter knew something; he must have been in the hall that next night, but for whose sake would he be silent? There was only one person he would risk so much to protect; the same person who went tapping through the hall with Ellen's cane to build an alibi—"

"That's a damned lie!" Douglas rose menacingly at Page's shouted words; Madeline sat as if frozen in her chair.

"No! No! It's not!" Juliet rose, too, her dark eyes larger than ever in her white face. "I wish it were, but it's not! You paid no attention to those bits from a letter that you found in the cellar; the only things that weren't burned. But I showed them to Myra and she told me whose writing they were, and she remembered the letter and told me that, too. It was written by Robert West, just before his wife died in an asylum for the insane. Then I knew—"

Douglas, sprang to shield her, with a warning cry, but his bandaged arm hampered him, and it was White who dragged back the screaming fury that was Madeline West. Then the screams ceased, and there was only insane laughter that echoed through the room as it will through our remembrance.

All along a doubt of Madeline had persisted in Juliet's mind, yet it seemed so reasonless that she would speak of it to no one. She herself had helped to establish Madeline's alibi, without any idea of being a dupe in the game. At times, it seemed to her that there was a hint of something abnormal in those dark eyes of Madeline's, but again she was silent. But she never forgot, or ceased trying to puzzle out that tragic secret mentioned by Ellen. It was some words of Trent's, she said, that first gave her the idea that she tried for a time to push aside.

Trent had spoken of Philip King's nervous instability; then she remembered the reiteration by persons who knew them, of his and Rose West's erratic, irresponsible natures, and that the first Mrs. King had died abroad. There was the combating of Ellen's marriage by her father; Ellen's own refusal to marry and her distress at her sister's marriage.

Why, Juliet wondered, was Ellen so disturbed by that marriage? Even if there was disgrace in the King family, which might be some day unearthed, that should not be the absolute impediment to Rose's marriage that Ellen seemed to believe it.

These were all vague, unformed suspicions when she was allowed to look at those two scraps of paper. And looking at them, she allowed her imagination full play, where we restrained ours.

The words, or parts of words: "hasty you would—" and again, "to warn us—" taken with the opening lines, "she is worse," seemed to her, significant.

Had not Ellen said something at the time of her sister's marriage about their being so hasty and her having been unable to warn them? She took the letter to Myra, and Myra broke down with a suddenness that was terrifying.

The letter was Robert West's; he had written it shortly before his wife died, when she was violently insane and it had been necessary to send her to an institution. Mrs. King had been "queer" for some time before they went to the foreign country where she was to be buried.

That was why they had gone away; Myra had never talked of it to Ellen or let her think that she knew. She would have told, she said, but Miss Ellen wouldn't have wanted her to, and she didn't see what good it would do.

But to Juliet the implications were instantly terrifyingly plain.

"Did Madeline know?"

She didn't think so, Myra said.

"Unless it was just lately. Miss Ellen wouldn't have let her marry anyone without telling them, and she wouldn't have wanted her to marry at all. She would have tried to keep her from it—"

Juliet left her then and went upstairs where I knocked, at her door and she pleaded with me to give her some time alone. Who would Walter keep silent for but Madeline! And hadn't Doug, or someone—said that perhaps Madeline knew who was in the hall that night or she would not have gone out?

We thought it might have been Walter whom Madeline surprised there; that she had been knocked down by someone was beyond doubt and seemed to put her still farther from suspicion. But suppose, Juliet thought now, it had been Madeline who locked the doors, her own included, and not knowing that she left a way for Walter to enter the hall through Mark's room?

She had met him and in the struggle was genuinely stunned, but from then on she was not safe. What she may have told him to allay his suspicions is only surmise; but he was madly in love with her, and I remembered too late the tone in which he had said:

"Fond of me? Well, that will do, I suppose, and you'll have a chance to prove it—"

But back to Juliet— She remembered again, pacing the bedroom nervously, something which had puzzled her before, and gone unexplained. When telling of her experience in the hall that night, Madeline had said:

"I didn't know then that all the doors were locked."

But none of us had talked to her then, and she had, by her own story, tried only Jack Page's door. How could she know that those doors were locked?

Then Juliet went back to the night of the murder, and the conviction grew on her that Madeline's visit to her had been too opportune, coming almost too soon after the closing of Ellen's door. And in spite of her protests that they should not trouble Ellen, she had not gone away until Ellen's death had been discovered and the impossibility of her having been the murderer established.

Why hadn't she gone to Ellen in the first place? Wouldn't it have been more natural? The questions rang in Juliet's brain remorselessly. A motive had puzzled her—she could not believe that the desire for mere financial independence would be enough. But if it was the loss of her lover that threatened and the loss of an eventual inheritance as well—

The first would be enough; she believed Madeline's love for Page to be as consuming as had been Walter King's for his cousin. "To my niece, Madeline West"—would that will have read "on condition that she never marry"? Then she heard Jackson and White come, and some uncanny sense warned her that she must speak soon.

From Madeline we never got a coherent story; her disintegration was complete and absolute; there was never a question or possibility of bringing her to trial. From her ravings that afternoon we pieced together a story that served, with what we knew and guessed.

Earlier that Friday evening, she had gone to Ellen as she said, and Ellen told her finally that she could not marry Page without telling him of the strain of insanity in the family, and that if she did marry she would be disinherited. That was enough to decide her, and later she crept to the window, armed with gun and silencer—the latter bought no one knows where.

She must have had some idea what was coming when she went to Hillside for the last time. The two shots fired,

she had unlatched the connecting door; the tall cabinet
had probably not been moved back into place. Then she
collected the papers from the desk, and I heard her stealing down the back stairs to burn them.

She must have been finishing her task when Mark came
home, heard a slight noise in the cellar and went down.
He has been able to talk only a little yet, but it was as we
guessed. He said:

"What are you burning?" and she sprang at him like a
tiger, her hand grasping the hatchet. She struck once and
his cry, "Don't! Don't!" was silenced by the second blow.
Then the time was short, or she believed him dead, and
she crept upstairs again.

There were other dark gowns in Ellen's closet, and she
must be prepared if someone saw her. Ellen's cane—and the
careful tapping with it down the hall and stairway, waking
Juliet as she intended, and the happy chance of her looking
down and testifying that she saw a figure below in the hall.

But the fingerprints must be and were removed from
the cane; the door locked on the inside, and she stepped
through the window and back through the hall to her own
room.

But during the day she must have grown uneasy about
Mark, and took the one opportunity that presented when
we thought her sleeping to slip into the cellar. Again chance
played into her hands, for Annie ran foolishly screaming
into the front hall and gave her barely time to run up the
back stairway, into her room again and join Juliet and me
by the time the outcry had penetrated upstairs.

Whichever of us said that Saturday night's performance
was a mad one gave the only reason that we can advance
for it. Perhaps she thought to frighten us; perhaps it ap-
pealed to her insane mind as humorous. It was easy to take
the key from the front door; to turn off the light switch
and lock us in.

The only flaw in the performance was Walter's appearance. She kept him, by some beguilement, from telling, but he had signed his death warrant when he came on her in the hall that night. Perhaps in the end cool reason told him to save his own skin, or he felt some prompting of danger and began to write a confession which he could hold over her head.

Where she got the poison is still unknown to us, but she had a friend in the city who was a chemist and she must have come prepared with more weapons than one. The powders that she substituted in her attempt to do away with Mark lest he recover and be able to talk lucidly before she could get away must have been the ones that Trent gave to Ellen.

It was she who took the diary; we found it hidden in her room.

For the rest, the homecoming of Philip King and Long's rash attack played into her hands by diverting the trend of investigation. But once she must have been stricken with panic, when Jackson's suspicion turned so definitely toward Page.

That was the one thing that she did not want; that would be fatal to her plans. Yet she kept her head even then, with her carefully calculated suggestions as to her own possible guilt and motive, and all the twisted cleverness of the insane.

Poor Trent's warning to Ellen was easily enough explained. She told him of her intention to keep Madeline and Jack from marrying, without telling her real reason. He said: "If you do it, you will be sorry," thinking only that it was not right to meddle with the lives of others, and his words stopped any further confidences she might have made.

Trent, "chivalrous" as Mrs. French had claimed, would not speak, conscious that he might be turning suspicion toward Madeline or Page. As to his vivacious widow, the engagement existed, as he said, only in her own mind. His allegiance to Ellen had never wavered and she knew it, but probably hoped to take advantage of that same chivalry by putting him in a position where he must affirm or ungallantly deny their engagement.

I "gave away" the bride at a quiet wedding a month ago and Juliet and Douglas run in and out often enough to keep me from brooding needlessly over the happenings I have recorded here. Philip and Mark King occupy the house at Hillside now, but it will be sold soon; Trent and Myra have gone away. It is for Page that I feel most sympathy; drifting about somewhere in the world, trying to forget Madeline West.

For additional
stories of adventure, fantasy,
mystery, fright, and fun, visit
CoachwhipBooks.com

VIRGINIA RATH

DEATH AT
DAYTON'S FOLLY

Details at
CoachwhipBooks.com

Available from your favorite online retailers

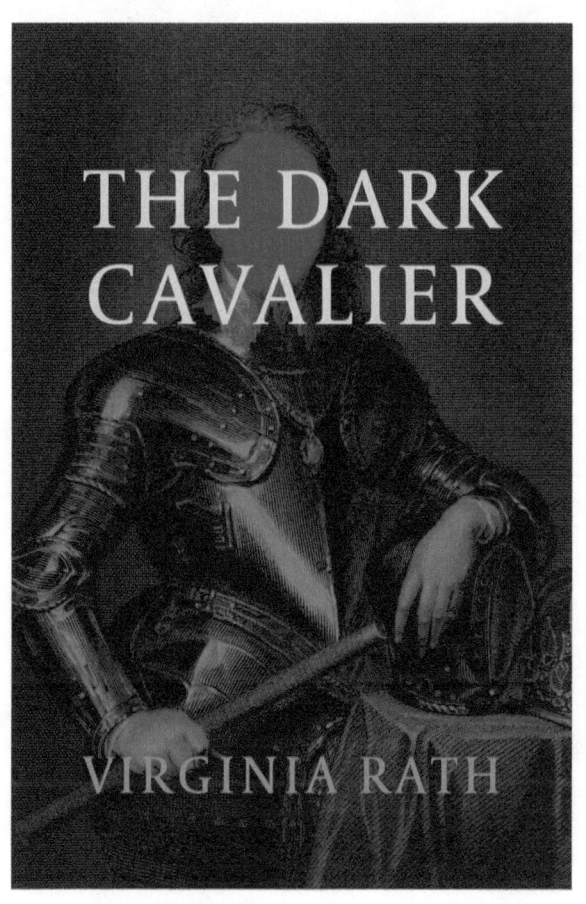

Details at
CoachwhipBooks.com

Available from your favorite online retailers

Death at
Windward Hill

Murder in the
French Room

HELEN JOAN HULTMAN

Details at
CoachwhipBooks.com

Available from your favorite online retailers

HELEN BURNHAM

THE MURDER OF
LALLA LEE

—

THE TELLTALE
TELEGRAM

Details at
CoachwhipBooks.com

Available from your favorite online retailers

DEATH
ON THE CAMPUS
ADDISON
SIMMONS

Details at
CoachwhipBooks.com

Available from your favorite online retailers

Details at
CoachwhipBooks.com

Available from your favorite online retailers

Details at
CoachwhipBooks.com

Available from your favorite online retailers

www.ingramcontent.com/pod-product-compliance
Lightning Source LLC
Chambersburg PA
CBHW020826260626
47169CB00003B/850